FIC Doole

Dooley, S.
Livvie Owen lived here.

Livvie Owen Lived Here

OWEN & HERE

BY SARAH DOOLEY

Feiwel and Friends
New York

A FEIWEL AND FRIENDS BOOK
An Imprint of Macmillan

Library of Congress Cataloging-in-Publication Data

Dooley, Sarah.
Livvie Owen lived here / Sarah Dooley. — 1st ed.
p. cm.
Summary: Fourteen-year-old Livvie Owen, who has autism, and her
family have been forced to move frequently because of her outbursts,
but when they face eviction again, Livvie is convinced she has a
way to get back to a house where they were all happy, once.
ISBN: 978-0-312-61253-5
[1. Autism—Fiction. 2. Family life—Fiction. 3. Schools—Fiction.] I. Title.
PZ7.D72652Li 2010
[Fic]—dc22
2010013009

Book design by Elizabeth Tardiff

Feiwel and Friends logo designed by Filomena Tuosto

First Edition: 2010

10 9 8 7 6 5 4 3 2 1

www.feiwelandfriends.com

For my students, who gave me this assignment

Livvie Owen Lived Here

Chapter 1

I heard the whistle blast at 9:15. Funny, the thought that struck me wasn't that the whistle had stopped blowing years ago, but that it should have blown at six. There was a time when the whistle was as reliable as the opening and closing of the hardware store or the passing of the ten o'clock train. The whistle used to rattle the windows and frighten the cats of Nabor every six a.m. and six p.m. for decades.

That was, as my parents liked to say, "way back when." Used to be, everybody in Nabor who didn't work at the hardware store worked at the paper mill, and the whistle told them when to come to work in the morning and when to go home at night. Then one day the whistle blew at six p.m. and everybody went home. The next morning, the whistle didn't blow, so nobody ever came back.

Nabor—with an A—is my town. Nabor is also the neighbor to Neighbor—with an E—which is the town everybody's heard of. Neighbor-with-an-E boasts a college and a Super Walmart and several law firms with names like Schubert and Schubert, and Williams and Williams, and the less-popular Williams and Schubert. Nabor-with-an-A? Well, Nabor-with-an-A boasts that it is Neighbor-with-an-E's neighbor. We've got a stoplight and two stop signs. A closed paper mill where the stray cats run wild.

And me. Olivia Owen. Former neighbor to just about everyone in Nabor.

You don't have to believe me. You can look. Open a door. Peek through a window. It almost doesn't matter which house you try; it won't take you more than a couple of blocks. You'll find *Livvie Owen Lived Here* written on the walls of over twenty dwellings in the county. It's the only sentence I ever learned how to write.

When the whistle blew, I was standing on a chair on my tiptoes, lining up drinking cups. I knew it was silly, but my eyes checked the microwave clock, glowing green across the dark kitchen at me. It really did say 9:15, not 6:00—neither time to go to work nor time to come home. I felt compelled then to check the calendar, just to make sure I had that part right as well. But it continued to list the proper year; nothing there had changed.

In the brief seconds it took me to confirm that nothing suspicious had happened with time, my fingers slipped on my mud mug and it dashed itself to the floor.

The whistle was still blowing when the sound of glass shattering raised the volume almost to unbearable. My ears didn't like so many levels of noise all at once. I wobbled on the chair, ready to fall, and felt familiar pressure building up inside my head. The mug looked so sad and betrayed on the floor, all scattered into pieces I was certain glue wouldn't fix. As the whistle faded into the night and the sound of glass gave way to the sound of my breathing and the clicking of the cooling stove, I curled my toes into the chair's woven seat and let my hands find their way into my hair.

"That did not happen!" I hollered into the darkened house. "That had just better not have happened, young lady! Don't you dare drop that mug, Livvie Owen! Hold on tight before the whistle blows!"

I held on tight to a lot of things, but lately it seemed like it was all the wrong ones. Like the cups. My family had so many different types of drinking cups that if I didn't keep them lined up neat, I could scarcely think about anything else. The chaos in the kitchen cupboards kept me distracted till I gave in and fixed it. My teachers called it "self-stimming" and made it sound like something bad, but I only wanted to put things right. There was nothing I could do about the mismatched collection of cups we owned, not with the high cost of sets of things. But at least I could give the cupboard a little peace by putting things in order the best I could manage.

I liked to put the glass cups on the top shelf. That way, when the cabinet was open and the sun was on, the light could catch the glass and sparkle. Plastic lived on the bottom according to color, left to right, starting with the cups that had words. With everything in order, I was always able to find my favorite cup, a glass coffee mug that felt like it was made out of hardened mud. It lived on the far right of the top shelf and I used it for everything from water to coffee to my morning yogurt, which was difficult to sip, but worth it if I got to use my mug. It felt worn and soothing under my hands.

When the mud mug hit the floor, the whistle got louder, like all noises did when I started to get upset. I remembered the whistle from my childhood—which is to say, I remembered being routinely frightened by a loud noise, and I remembered my mother saying, "Little Livvie, it's just the paper mill whistle. You're all right." My mother was always saying, "You're all right." She said it to me when I got upset. Said it to my father when he stopped laughing and got forehead crinkles, which was usually when I was being difficult or when the bills came in before his paycheck.

Back when there really *was* a whistle, she said it to the cats each time they went tearing out of the kitchen and slid under the sofa we used to have, the green one with all the stripes that made my eyes dizzy. They hid under that sofa every time the whistle blew. You would think after a while they would get used to it, but they never did. I think maybe they just wanted an excuse to be afraid, like my big sister reading ghost stories in the dark.

Or maybe it was something about the whistle itself that stopped them from getting used to it. It *was* a scary whistle, high and low at the very same time: a shrill note piercing a sky you imagined was dark from smoke and chemicals, then sewn up with a dark, heavy note like an angry cat's growl, a note that made my stomach feel hollow.

Coupled with shattering glass, the noise was unbearable, and my hands slapped over my ears. My mug didn't pick itself up, so I jumped down off the chair to get it. That's when I remembered it was made out of glass, and glass is sharp. Crashing backward and knocking over the chair, I

tumbled to the kitchen floor and grabbed my bleed-
ing foot.

"That did not happen!" I bellowed again. "Glass
is sharp, young lady! You watch your step!"

"Oh, lord," I heard my mother murmur, and her
bedroom door opened. "Livvie, is there glass? Come
away, honey." A light switched on.

I blinked up at my mother and hollered, "The
paper mill blew its whistle at the wrong time! It's
supposed to be at six! It made Livvie drop her mug
and Livvie is very angry!"

My mother quickly took in the scene around her
and grabbed a dish towel off the counter. She wrapped
it around my foot and held it there. I watched her, but
I couldn't feel the cut anymore. I was too busy fighting
off my overwhelming fury at the whistle.

"Simon!" Karen called. Although her voice was
just as loud as mine, my mother never hollered or bellowed. She sounded gentle even with her voice raised,
as polished as I was rough, my father, Simon, said
sometimes.

"Three hours and fifteen minutes late!" I yelled
at my mother. "Why was the paper mill whistling so
late, Karen? It's supposed to blow at six and six!"
I got louder with every word and I heard someone
shuffle in the doorway.

"Livvie, shut *up*!" my little sister, Lanie, yelled,

skidding into the kitchen in her socks and her purple pajamas. "I'm trying to sleep! I have the science fair tomorrow!" Her pale hair stood up in sleepy patches, and her eyes were narrow.

"You tell that whistle to shut up! That's who should shut up!" I yelled back, slamming against the cabinets and jarring the silverware in its tray. Underneath my noise I heard Karen's soft voice explaining to my sister, "She's hurt herself. *Simon!* Lanie, get your father."

Lanie took one look at my foot, and her eyes widened in horrified fascination. She dashed for my parents' room, screeching at a volume rivaling my own, "Daddy! Come and see! Livvie's cut her foot off!"

I heard shuffling, quite a bit faster than my father usually traveled, before he appeared beside my mother looking winded. "What's all the hollering?"

"Liv dropped her mug and stepped on it." Karen handed my injured foot to my father and scooted around to hug me from behind. Karen was much better with words and hugs than blood. "The girl was up on a chair at this hour, stimming on the glasses."

"It was the whistle's fault!" I hollered, because nobody seemed to be listening. Or understanding. Sometimes words that made perfect sense in my head simply would not spit out in the proper order.

"The mill whistle blew and it wasn't six! It was three hours and fifteen minutes late and it made Livvie drop her mug!" I wrapped my hands in my hair and tugged, feeling the pressure inside me ease as though I were pulling on a cork.

"Livvie, stop that!" Karen swatted gently at my hands. "Stop it. You're all right."

"I am not all right, I'm angry!" I yelled. "The whistle blew wrong!"

"What whistle?" Lanie grumped, blowing her long hair impatiently out of her face. "I didn't hear a whistle!"

My gaze traveled to her, but she wasn't lying. I could tell by her nose not crinkling. So I checked my parents and they were looking at each other with concern and dismay on their faces, two emotions I had a lot of practice understanding.

Fear shook my hands loose from my hair and made me cold. I wrapped my arms around myself tightly. "Only Livvie heard the whistle?" I ventured. My old teacher Miss Mandy worked with me a lot on third person versus first person, back before she ran away. First person was when I said "I" and "me" instead of calling myself "Livvie," and I was supposed to use first person all the time, just like I was supposed to call Karen and Simon "Mom" and "Dad." Only sometimes when I got upset, it made more sense

8

just to use the proper names for people so everybody knew who was who.

"I didn't hear anything but glass breaking and then you," Karen said in a shaky voice, one that underlined just how frightened she had been when she heard those noises. "Simon?"

The way she asked, I knew she was humoring me, knew that if Simon couldn't hear a kid banging around and breaking glass all over the floor, he definitely couldn't hear a whistle that, apparently, was imaginary. "No, honey. I didn't hear any whistle."

My eyes blinked back and forth, but my parents weren't lying, either. I could tell by their eyes not moving away from mine. So mine did the moving instead, rolling up to the cupboard, which now had an empty spot on the far right side of the top shelf. I started squeezing my joints tight, first my shoulders, then my elbows, then my wrists, all the way down to my toes, trying to use the technique Miss Mandy taught me to relax when I got upset.

After a few minutes, a breath went out of me and then I felt less pressure, maybe like I wouldn't explode now. I let myself lean back against Karen and relaxed my muscles a little.

"Ouch," I said faintly.

"I'll bet," my mother said, planting a kiss on top of my forehead.

"I didn't mean to wake you," I said to Lanie.

She sniffed. "Whatever. Don't do it again. I have stuff to do." I heard her feet shuffling with impatience all the way back to the bedroom.

My mother stroked my hair back out of my face and dropped another kiss on top of me. "She's just nervous about her science fair," she said. "Don't worry about it, honey."

"What were you doing standing on a chair in the middle of the night?" my father's somewhat-less-sympathetic voice asked from his place at my foot.

"Oh." I forgot about that part. "It's not really the middle of the night. It's only a little after nine. I started thinking about how Lanie did the dishes, and she never does the cups right. I couldn't sleep."

"Well, I think your old folks were right about standing on chairs not being safe," my father said. I loved him for a lot of reasons, but one of them was because that was *all* he said. Lying on the floor with a dish towel around my foot and the remains of my mug scattered around me on the floor, I could easily see what a stupid idea it was to stand on a chair in the middle of the night. It was seeing these situations from the other end, before they happened, that was the hard part. Apparently, you just never knew when an imaginary factory whistle was going to startle you into breaking something.

My father finished wrapping my foot and hooked his arms under mine, lifting me onto my good foot. "Well, I think you're going to live," he announced. Then added drily, "I think the floor's going to make it, too."

"Don't move," my mother said, perhaps a little more sharply than she intended, when I started to hobble toward my room. "Let me get the broom."

Before I could answer, the trailer jumped with the force of a firm knock on the door. We all three tensed again and nobody moved for a minute.

Unless we were expecting a package or we'd moved next door to someone good at baking, a knock on the door almost never meant anything good. Sometimes it was the guy in khaki who came to shut off the water. Other times it was the neighbor complaining because my cats got loose in their yard.

Tonight it was one of two people, and neither one of them was welcome. It was either Glenna from one door down, or it was Janna from one door up.

"Please be Glenna!" I hollered as Simon finally moved to answer the door. Karen shushed me. The door opened and the first thing to blow in on the stiff October wind was three orange leaves.

The second was not Glenna. It was Janna and she wasn't smiling.

"Good evening," my father said formally, and I

11

wished he slept in something other than his boxers and a T-shirt. I felt my face get red.

"Simon," Janna said with a stiff nod for my father. Then, glancing at my mother, "Karen." Her eyes slipped over the top of me without focusing. My eyes were more than happy to avoid her, too. Her stern lips and thin cheeks made me queasy.

"Bed," Karen said firmly before Janna could say anything else. With her hands on my shoulders, she steered me around the broken glass. I limped on the tiptoe of my injured foot and hobbled down the hallway toward my bedroom, casting a nervous glance over my shoulder as I did. Simon offered Janna a chair, and she refused. Her sweatpants had stains. I didn't like the way she was frowning.

Karen looked at me lovingly as she led me to my room, but there were other emotions all tangled up in the creases around her eyes. I couldn't name them all. Miss Mandy liked to tell me it was okay not to know the names of all the emotions I saw, but I didn't like not knowing the names for things. I liked names. I liked to memorize lists of them. These emotions weren't simple like the happy and sad and angry flash cards Miss Mandy liked to show me. They didn't make flash cards for this.

"Sweet girl, please don't get up again tonight," my mother pleaded.

I felt an uneasy feeling in my stomach that I think was called guilt. This one was familiar enough I had a name for it. "I promise," I said quickly.

Her smile looked tired. "Good girl."

"Hey, Kar—Mom?" She accepted me calling her Karen, but sometimes joy got crinkled up in her eyes when I called her Mom, so I tried to remember. "Was there really not a whistle?"

"I don't know, darling. I just didn't hear anything."

" 'Cause I heard it loud and clear. Just like at the Sun House. Six and six."

She smiled and kissed my forehead one final time. Then turned on my fish lamp and turned off my big light. She piled my nine blankets on top of me so I felt weighted down enough to sleep.

"Good night, Livvie-bug."

"Good night, Karen."

Only, tonight I couldn't sleep, not with Janna's voice going on in the kitchen, loud enough to hear over the familiar whir of my fish lamp. I turned on my side and watched the little plastic speckled fish swim endless circles around their tiny swath of fake ocean. I wanted to hear the ocean, like Tasha showed me in a seashell once. Instead I heard Janna and caught the words "inconsiderate" and "out of control."

Not quite forgetting my promise to Karen, but hiding it in the back of my thoughts, I slipped from my bed just behind her and crept down the hallway to listen. Janna was pretending to be patient. I knew she was pretending because she was talking faster than usual and I could hear a note of stress in her voice.

"When you first rented," she said, "you told me she was better. After last time, I thought . . . but you told me she was better, and I took you at your word."

"She *is* better," Karen said quickly, as though offended about something.

"She doesn't *sound* better."

"It doesn't happen overnight, ma'am," Simon said. Anyone else might have thought he was calm, but I could hear the venom in his tone. "She's *better*, not *cured*. There haven't been any miracles, but she's grown up a lot and she has more self-control than she used to." I sort of felt like I had swallowed something cold. I didn't like hearing them discuss me this way.

"Well, see that she manages to control herself at this hour in the future," Janna said stonily. "Half the neighborhood is awake and if they complain to me, I'm going to have to complain to you."

"Have a nice night, Janna," Simon said firmly, and I heard him close the door behind her. Immediately, he began to swear, running his hands through his graying hair over and over. I knew he was doing it because he always did. My mother shushed him and got the broom.

"You're all right," she said softly.

"I'm going to start looking out of town," he answered, beginning to pace the length of the kitchen. I could hear the linoleum creaking under him, back and forth across the darkened room. "I'm going to have to."

"Oh, we're not there yet," Karen said briskly. I heard stitches pulling and knew she was picking at her robe. It had almost no embroidery left anymore.

"Are we going to wait until we *are* there before we deal with it?" Simon asked tiredly. "If we lose this place, we're not going to find another one in Nabor. We've burnt all our damn bridges."

I waited for Karen to tell him he was wrong. Not finding a place in Nabor meant living someplace else. Not acceptable.

"But Livvie loves it here, Simon. We all do."

His voice got longer like the shadows down the hallway. "I can't always make everybody happy. We have to eat, Kar. We have to have a roof. If it's a roof in another town, well, it's still a roof and we still have to have one."

She didn't answer and I wasn't sure I knew how to,

either. The tiles and the floorboards and the sidewalks of Nabor had been my home my entire life. I couldn't imagine living anywhere else. Slipping quickly back into my room, I burrowed under my nine blankets and had a serious discussion with myself.

"Livvie, you cannot do this again," I whispered. "You have to control yourself."

From deep inside me, a response wisped up like smoke, but it was only another question.

"Shush," I answered in the darkness. "I don't *know* how. You're just going to have to do it."

Chapter 2

Heavy blankets were what Karen would call "a mixed blessing." Heavy was good because it held me down to the bed and made me sleep. It was also bad because it made it difficult for me to jump awake in the morning and escape my scary dreams.

This morning my kicking feet made me remember quick that one of them was hurt. The events of the night before came flooding back, and my fingers clenched involuntarily as though trying to recapture my coffee mug.

"Oh, crap, what am I going to drink my yogurt out of this morning?" I mumbled to the plastic fish swimming circles by my ear.

It was my experience that whatever sentence I happened to say upon waking set the tone for the rest of the day. If it was a good sentence—something like "No school today" or "Wow, Lanie, you look like you're in a good mood"—I could count on having a good day.

But if it was something bad—something like "Lanie, get out of my face" or "Oh, crap, what am I going to drink my yogurt out of this morning?"—I could pretty much count on a crummy day to follow.

I started blowing through pursed lips, hard. Sometimes doing breaths like this made the frustration stop building up inside me and the pressure never got big enough that I needed to let it out another way. As long as I could remember, the pressure had been there, but it got a lot bigger the year the whistle stopped blowing. Miss Mandy liked to talk with me about it, insisting that by talking, I gained ownership, which I think meant I was supposed to be able to make the pressure go away when I wanted.

"A lot of people who have autism," she said, "have something similar to this pressure of yours. But they learn to control it and you can do the same. Just breathe with me." She would take several deep breaths, blowing out through her lips. Her breaths made her teased bangs wobble. When I did it, my tangles got tangled up further and my bangs brushed my forehead, making me shiver. "There now. Isn't that better?"

I said the words to myself as I worked on getting calm. "There now, Livvie. Isn't that better?" After a minute, I was calm enough to peel off my nine blankets one at a time. My bandage had shifted a little in the night and blood had seeped onto my sheet. I covered it up quick with the blanket so I wouldn't have to look at it; I didn't like seeing spots on things. Squirming out of bed, I limped across the flattened carpet to stand on the metal heat vent on my one good foot. The metal dug stripes into the bottom of my foot, but it was worth it to catch every breath of warm air the aging trailer could cough out.

Properly warmed, I stuck my good foot in its slipper and adjusted the bracelet on my wrist. The bracelet used to be a kitten's collar, back when Orange Cat was little enough to fit into it. The jingling ID tag was still attached, and my remaining cat, Gray Cat, came skittering out from under the bed, hoping for a jingle toy. Halfway across my room, her claws caught the carpet and she skidded to a stop, staring in horror at the fuzzy slippers that I wore every single day. She never stopped being afraid of them.

"You're silly, Gray Cat," I informed her, stretching my arms above my head to get awake. Hopping on my one good foot, I headed for the kitchen, where I found Lanie pacing tiny circles on the green linoleum. Lanie spent a lot of time in the mornings getting ready, for a kid who was only in middle school. It was my first year of high school and I didn't spend half as much time, preferring to use my time wisely, petting Gray Cat or thumbing through a real estate catalog.

Lanie cleared her throat and faced the sink, which I think was her imaginary audience. "The reason I chose this topic for the science fair is because I wanted to make a difference in the way people perceive mice. Mice are not such bad creatures once you get to know—would you stop hopping? Once you get to know them." She cleared her throat importantly. "Meet Bentley. Bentley is a mouse, but that doesn't stop him from being a caring and considerate friend. Bentley is also quite smart. He is— would you *stop hopping, please?*—he is able to find his way through a complicated maze to get to the— *Mom! Make Olivia stop hopping! She's driving me crazy!*"

"I *have* to hop!" I hollered back. "I cut my foot last night and I can't walk on it! How am I supposed to get to breakfast if I don't hop?"

"You could always starve," Lanie snapped. "Mom, make her stop hopping so close to Bentley! If you knock over his cage, he'll get loose and your stupid cat will eat him, and then I'll have to eat your stupid cat!"

"*Karen!*" I bellowed. "*Lanie's going to eat my cat!*"

"Girls!" Karen came into the kitchen, also hopping, pulling on her slipper with one hand and balancing herself on the door frame with the other. "Please get your breakfast and sit down without killing each other. Just one morning I'd like to not have to plot how I'm going to hide the bodies. *Simon!* Natasha's not awake yet and it's your turn!" Slipper in place, she lowered her other foot to the floor and shuffled to the counter to start the coffee.

"But, Mom, she almost knocked over Bentley!"

"No mice at the breakfast table," Karen said firmly without looking. Then, just as firmly, "No cats at the breakfast table, either." I didn't know how she knew I had just picked up Gray Cat and snuck her onto my lap, but I quickly set her down again and folded my hands on the table. After last night's adventures, I didn't want to get myself into any extra trouble.

My father came stumbling out of the bedroom moments later, his glasses crooked and his chin dark with stubble. His hair stood up on the pillow side and his eyes were rimmed with red. Pulling his sweater on over his head, he shuffled toward Natasha's room with an audible yawn.

It would be a while before he returned. I never understood how Natasha managed to sleep so soundly, sharing a room with Lanie as she did, but then Tash was the quietest of all us Owens, anyway. Especially lately. She used to break her silence long enough to laugh and joke sometimes, and always to yell at Lanie if Lanie was mean to me. But lately all she did was read and eat, mostly in that order.

Her reading used to be a good thing. She used to read to me every day, the same three books over and over. She said it was like visiting an old friend, sweet and familiar. I could read to myself, but not very good. Mostly just -*at* and -*op* and -*ug* words and they didn't make much sense when you strung them together in a sentence. My parents read, too, but they did the voices and the faces as if I was a little kid, stringing words into a story even Lanie was too old for. The way Natasha strung words together, they painted beautiful stories on the insides of my eyelids. They made me feel like I was part of the story, as if I was one of the pages turning. I could feel the warm words, the way they felt as they were read, released from the pressure of their pages.

But Natasha hadn't been reading to me lately. I

wasn't sure why, but it had something to do with Orange Cat.

Natasha stumbled in to fix herself a bagel, plopping half on the table in front of me. Crumbs scattered and I wrinkled my nose, meticulously wiping them away. Orange Cat's baby collar jingled on my wrist and I caught Lanie glaring.

"What'd you do to your foot, Liv-long-and-prosper?" Natasha asked. It was one of her goofy nicknames for me that made me uneasy when I was a little kid and made me giggle now.

"I broke my mug and stepped on it." I picked at the bagel. I really wanted yogurt, but there was nothing to drink it out of.

"Your mud mug?" She gave me a quick glance. I think the look there was called sympathy. "I'm sorry, hon."

"It was stupid." I shrugged. "I shouldn't have been climbing on the chair, but also the whistle shouldn't have blown."

"Yeah, that was weird, huh?" Natasha agreed. "Somebody must have been fooling around at the old factory."

Eyes roved around the table—mine, Lanie's, my parents'—everyone but Natasha's. Hers stayed cluelessly on her book, just above her bagel.

"You mean you—you heard that?" I asked faintly

when it appeared the rest of my family was not going to ask.

"Yeah, it was weird. It sounded just like it used to back at the Sun House. It was like old times." She smiled quickly up at the table, then looked up again at length when she realized we were all still staring at her.

"What?" she asked with something funny in her voice that I thought might be called guilt. "Livvie always says she misses the Sun House. Why can't I?"

"I guess there really was a whistle," Simon breathed to Karen.

I felt something bubble up in my stomach too suddenly for me to put a name to it. My hands clenched up and I wrinkled my forehead. "How come you believe it when Tash says it? I told you I heard it, but just because Lanie didn't—"

"That's because they know I'm sensible," Lanie said in what she pretended was a helpful voice. "You're fanciful. That's something different. It means you might be making up a whistle, but *I* would tell the truth."

I slapped my bagel back down on my plate, making Natasha's fork jump out of the cream cheese tub and clatter on the table. "I always tell the truth! And Tash heard it, too, so who's the liar now, huh?

You must have heard it! You share a room with Tash and she heard it!"

"The only thing I heard was you banging and hollering in the middle of the night when Bentley and I needed our sleep!"

"You and stupid Bentley!" I stood up and slammed my chair back so hard it hit the counter. Bentley's cage rocked dangerously. "Why don't you just go marry him?"

"Olivia!" My father fixed me with a stare that made my insides feel like I had swallowed something slimy. "Have a seat, young lady."

"But—" I stomped and pointed at Lanie. She stomped back and crossed her arms over her chest, turning her back squarely to me. Usually Lanie proclaimed herself too old for such behavior, but I seemed uniquely able to bring it out in her.

My father held up his hand to silence both of us, then turned to Lanie. "Melanie, please stop picking at your sister."

"But she—" She pointed back at me.

Natasha grabbed Lanie's pointing finger and folded it back to her side, under the table so Karen and Simon couldn't see. "Honey," she said to me calmly while Lanie struggled to get free. "What time did you hear that whistle?"

"Precisely nine-fifteen," I said in kind of a small voice. With Natasha's calm gaze on me, I remembered how important it was now not to have outbursts. I was forever remembering things too late.

"Well, that's funny, 'cause I was asleep," Natasha said. "But I definitely heard it."

Lanie yanked her hand away with a huff, but she didn't point or say anything else. This, coupled with Natasha's words, finally made it possible for me to settle back into my chair. If Natasha believed me, it didn't matter what Lanie thought. I scooted my chair farther away from Lanie's.

"So, what are you doing at school today, Livvie?" My mother was halfway through her coffee and still blinking sleep out of her eyes. She looked eager to steer the conversation in a new direction.

"I don't know, not much," I grumped. "The new sub is stupid. But the speech therapist said she would come and get me and we can play UNO."

"What's wrong with the new sub this time?" Lanie asked. "Is her hair the wrong color, or does she just not like putting up with all your—"

"Melanie Elizabeth!" Simon sat back with a thump and pointed at the sink. "Get your dishes rinsed. Get your mouse. Get going. Now."

"But I'm not finished with my—"

"*Now!*"

Lanie sighed a loud, dramatic sigh, the kind Miss Mandy used to say was impolite when I did it to her and Mr. Raldy. "Fine," she grumbled. "Don't mind me. I'm going to go win one for science. Just see if I share my prize money with any of you crazy people." She banged out of the room with Bentley swinging in his cage.

I took a last bite of my bagel—bringing the grand total of bites I'd taken to three—and dumped the rest in the trash. Turning back to the table, I caught Natasha staring.

"You used to eat," she observed drily. "Do you remember those days?"

"I eat," I said defensively.

"Three bites. When you were a baby, you always finished first. Then you launched yourself mouth-first at whatever was still left on my plate. Usually pumpkin pie." Turning to our parents, she added, "Does it seem like we had pumpkin pie a lot back then?"

"Your grandmother gave us about eighteen cans of pie filling that winter." Karen drained her coffee mug and rolled her shoulders to wake up. "I think it must have been on sale. Either that or expired. We used to eat it on crackers. It was better than the canned meat—that's the other thing she gave us."

My father whisked his plate and coffee cup to

the sink. "I'm going to pretend I don't hear you talking about my mother," he said in a joking sort of voice. Joking voices, I was pretty good at recognizing, after years of growing up with my parents and my sisters. It was the more serious emotions I had a hard time labeling. The ones my family didn't talk about.

Chapter 3

Simon eyed Lanie and me warily as we piled into the car, but we were finished fighting, mostly. Lanie grabbed the front seat and I huffed a sigh and settled into the back, next to Simon's Walmart apron. Karen was off today and would pick us up on foot, me from the high school and Lanie from her car pool. These were my favorite days because Karen never made us walk straight home. We roamed up through the pinewoods or down to the swings at the elementary school. Sometimes we wound through downtown Nabor to buy an ice cream at the U-Save.

Natasha waved a peaceful-looking good-bye from her bike as she pedaled down the drive. Even in winter, Natasha loved to bike to school if we lived close enough. I watched her go, wistfully. I would love nothing more than to bike to school—my hair, which

I pictured longer and thinner in my daydreams, drifting back in the gentle wind, eyes watering with the cold, but in a good way. It would sure beat sitting here in this backseat behind Lanie, listening to her huff and sigh and yawn giant fake yawns that made my ears dizzy.

There was a time, way back—not quite as way back as the Sun House, but almost—when Lanie and I were friends. Not when she was a baby. When she was a baby, she was so loud she hurt my ears, and she always had Karen's and Simon's attention when she wanted it, while they told me to be a big girl and they would help me in a little while. Sometimes I bounced Lanie on my knee with Simon's help, and sometimes Karen let me hold her in the rocking chair, but mostly she was a change in my life that I just didn't feel ready for.

Around the time Lanie was born, I pulled out such a big chunk of my hair that my scalp bled. My parents were horrified. They rushed me to the hospital, like there was anything the hospital could do about a stupid missing chunk of hair. For a while after that, they made me keep my hair cut short. It was only lately they started letting me grow it out again, long like Natasha's, only too thick and not as pretty.

But when Lanie was one year and five months

old, something changed in our relationship. Around that time, she started speaking a language I could sort of understand, all about the colors and the motions of things. Her speech was visible. I could see the words she said because they made so much sense to me. It surprised me to learn that my family couldn't understand her. Her words were like pictures painted on the air. We spent all our time together.

I wasn't sure exactly when our friendship started to fade. Maybe when she said her first sentence that made sense to our parents. Maybe when Natasha started to understand her. And then there was the matter of the neighbor girl in one of the places we lived. The neighbor girl was my age, but she acted different. And Lanie liked her better.

By the time Lanie began speaking in clear, complete sentences to the people around her, she had stopped making sense to me. And it was as if she had forgotten I had ever made any sense to her.

"Try not to fall off any more chairs," Lanie said nastily as I climbed out of the car at my school. I stuck my tongue out at her and slammed the car door. Even though she thought she was too old for things like that, I still saw her stick her tongue out as the car pulled away. She would be riding with my father as far as Neighbor's city limits, where her science and mathematics middle school was located.

Her stupid Bentley mouse had helped her win a scholarship last year.

I stayed exactly where Simon left me until I saw Natasha pull up on her bike. Locking it to the rack, she slung an arm through mine the way we always did. We strolled through the courtyard, me hopping when necessary, stepping over book bags students had dropped in their rush to play horseshoes and four square and to huddle in groups to talk. I didn't like the way they looked at me as I passed— a fake smile here, a nervous look there. The problem was, they were always looking. I stuck my hands in my pockets and worried the lining of my sweater until the threads came loose in my fingertips. I clenched and unclenched my joints, starting with my shoulders. Rolled my head around in a circle on my neck. Hummed a little to myself, the same note over and over.

"Why so stressed today?" Natasha asked as we approached my classroom door.

"Stupid Lanie," I replied. "She's got Livvie all upset."

"She doesn't mean anything," Natasha answered. "She's eleven. That's why she's so mean. That's what eleven-year-olds do."

"You weren't mean when you were eleven," I pointed out.

"I was to Lanie," Natasha confided. "A million years ago, you know."

"Uh-uh, it was not a million years ago, it was five."

Tash smiled. "I know. It just *feels* like a million." With a sympathetic wave for my substitute teacher, she left me at the classroom door.

Mrs. Paxton was one of those substitutes you'd rather they would substitute for somebody else. Today was her fourth day and she was finally confident enough to smile, the kind with too much lipstick all around it, instead of scrutinizing me like I was about to attack her. Something about her behavior made me think my reputation preceded me, but she managed not to say it. She only patted me uncomfortably. She was a skinny lady with hair that was so white-blond it made my eyes feel dizzy. I moved away from her by several steps and watched her frown.

My school was a funny place. It had classrooms for the other kids, the ones who attended regular subjects like algebra and art. Instead of a classroom, we had this whole wing of our own, like maybe what we had was catching, which wasn't true except for Robert, who always had a cold. He liked card tricks and was pretty talented, according to Mrs. Paxton. To me, his tricks were flat. I could see how they were going to end from the start.

Our wing held two classrooms and no teachers. I think that said something about our wing. Word around the school was that we were so awful to our subs, they all ran away. By some accounts, we chased a couple of them clear out of the subbing profession. At least we managed to hang on to our classroom assistant, Mr. Raldy, for what it was worth. Mr. Raldy was exactly eight months from retirement. I knew because he kept a countdown written on the calendar on his desk, and Bristol, who could read best, liked to keep us all updated. Mr. Raldy was a tall man with a ring of white hair and almost none in the middle. He wore patterned sweaters and he had a hard time hearing us. Having Mr. Raldy was like having a picture hanging on the wall, keeping watch over us; he was not a man who interacted much.

I was not very good at friends, but that was okay because Georgia was. She called herself "G" because it was easiest to say, and that's all she said, all day long. "G. G. G." Not because it was her name but because it was her favorite letter. I liked that, because G was my favorite musical note. G always thought it was funny when I told her. She laughed and laughed when I told her I was going to sing G.

Besides Robert, Bristol, G, and me, there were two other kids in our classroom. Michael was skinny and quiet and got mad really easy, kind of like me, only all he ever talked about was snakes. Still, me and him were a lot alike, just the way Robert and Bristol were a lot alike. They were both what Robert's mother called "social butterflies." Bristol's thing was colors, but she didn't like to paint with them. She liked to wear them. Red and orange and yellow—her warm colors, she called them—on happy days, and green and blue and purple—her cool colors—on sad days. When Bristol was wearing cool colors like today's blue sweater, I knew to stay out of her way. When she was wearing warm colors, she hurt my eyes, so overall I didn't spend much time with Bristol.

There was also Peyton, who was silent. I was curious about Peyton. Most of us had been in class together since preschool, but Peyton had only joined us this year and she hadn't made any moves to get to know us. She used a wheelchair that I was pretty sure ran on batteries or something, because she just had to push a switch with her chin to make it move. Only she wasn't very interested in doing that and usually somebody else had to do it for her. Peyton had long hair that was the absolute prettiest color of brown. It made me think of warm earth in summer. I wanted to run my fingers through it, but the one time I did, way back in August, Mr. Raldy thought I was hair-pulling and took away my real estate books. I kept my distance from Peyton these days, just to be safe.

When I hobbled into the classroom, G galloped up to me with her short hair bouncing. Everything about G was short and bouncy.

"What's up, G?" I asked, slinging an arm around her shoulder. G beamed at me and snatched a picture off the key chain on her belt loop. She slapped it onto a strip of Velcro and handed it to me. I squinted at it. It was a picture of a TV.

"It's only Monday," I said, disappointed. "We can't do that today."

She nodded vigorously and pointed to the sub. Then to Robert and Bristol, huddled in a corner, whispering. A slow grin slid onto my face. Robert and Bristol had a lot of talents, but one was that they could usually convince the sub of just about anything they wanted. How was she to know we didn't usually watch our reward movie on Mondays? Or that we hadn't earned a reward this week? Mr. Raldy was good about not ratting us out to the sub. Took too much energy, I think.

Ripping "movie" off the Velcro strip, G replaced it with a cartoon picture of a girl laughing. I grinned back.

"Me, too," I agreed. "In fact, that makes me *very*

happy. That's just what I need to get over the frustrations of last night and this morning."

"What frustrations?" Bristol asked, even though I wasn't talking to her. I glared at her a little, but I still answered. Hobbling forward to shove my book bag into my cubby, I explained about the broken mug and the glass in my foot, then about my fight with my sister.

I didn't tell them about the factory whistle because it seemed like a lie, out in the daylight. But I did ask Michael, who had awesome hearing, whether he heard anything funny last night.

"I heard a lot of funny things," he told me. "I heard the channel seven news guy. He's funny. I heard the channel seven news guy and the channel sixteen news guy. I switched back and forth between the two of them. They were both making jokes about the president. The president and the—and the—and the Congress. I heard a lot of funny things. What did you have in mind?"

"I didn't mean funny like it made you laugh. I meant funny the way my sister means it, like funny-weird."

"Funny means it makes you laugh."

"Okay, well, did you hear anything weird last night?"

"I heard a lot of weird things. My dad snoring. My sister talking on the phone to her boyfriend. She made smoochy noises. That was very weird."

"Michael, focus!" I stepped into his line of vision and he blinked up at me.

"What should I focus on?"

"Did you hear a whistle last night?"

"My aunt Jacob whistles. I hate when my aunt Jacob whistles."

I rolled my eyes. "You don't have an aunt Jacob! Now pay attention!"

"I do too, kind of. I have an aunt Jenny and an uncle Jacob, but they do all the same things at all the same times, so it makes more sense to refer to them by fewer names. That way I'm not wasting my own time, which is better spent with snakes. Aunt Jacob means Aunt Jenny and Uncle Jacob, both of them together. They both whistle. I don't like when they whistle. It makes my ears feel weird. See, *weird*. Not funny. Funny would mean my ears laugh, and my ears don't laugh. They just buzz a little bit when my aunt Jacob whistles."

"Michael!" I stomped my foot. I felt like my own ears were starting to buzz a little bit. "What I want to know is whether you heard the factory whistle at the paper mill last night!"

There was a sudden silence in the special education wing. Silences were rare in this end of the building, and suddenly I felt very embarrassed. Just how loud had I been talking?

"The factory doesn't have a whistle anymore," Michael said logically.

I backpedaled quickly. "Okay. Okay. I was just checking. I guess I dreamed it."

"You dreamt about the factory whistle?" Bristol asked. "That's funny."

"No, it's weird," I corrected her impatiently.

G tapped my arm and handed me her Velcro strip. The pictures were of a girl sleeping with an empty thought bubble above her head, and a happy giraffe.

I smiled at G. "You had the giraffe dream again?" She had this recurring dream about a giraffe laughing and walking on a tightrope. Sometimes I wished I could be G for just a day.

She nodded with a big grin and rolled her eyes.

"I wish I could borrow your dream, G. Mine was weird."

She patted me sympathetically, then skipped off to her desk to set it up for the day. G had a very specific routine she went through before she could start her morning work. She had to have everything just so. Sometimes, when I thought of it, I felt bad G had to have a desk next to mine. Even though they were study carrels and she couldn't see my mess from her chair, I thought maybe she could sense it because it was so noticeable. My desk was littered with forgotten worksheets, half-colored coloring sheets, stickers Miss Mandy had let me earn that the subs weren't sure how to use right, and the parts of the newspaper left over after I cut out my real estate ads.

The real estate ads themselves, I pasted neatly in my blue notebook. The pretty houses gazed out at me from the pages, windows empty with promise.

There was one other thing on my desk, and I kept this in the center, although my mess was harder to contain when it was pushed around the edges. Facedown in the center of the study carrel was my picture of Orange Cat, the only one I hadn't put in a box and made Karen hide in the closet. I kept it close in case I needed to see him, but facedown because I couldn't bear to look him in the eye.

Orange Cat had been gone two months and I had looked at the picture only once. The day he left the world, I stared at his eyes in the photo, eyes so orange they were warm to look at. Sunset had nothing on Orange Cat. Orange Cat was a baby when I was Lanie's age. He was three years and two weeks when he slipped out the door after one of my tantrums and never came back.

I didn't look for him soon enough. I was upset before he left, about something stupid like toast crumbs in the butter, but it was nothing compared to how upset I was once I realized he was gone. It was the closest I had come to losing hair in years. I just couldn't believe that I couldn't go a couple of minutes back in time, if I really thought about it hard enough, and close the door more carefully. I melted down on the kitchen floor and by the time I found myself again, it was after twelve and Simon put me to bed, no arguments.

The next day was too late. All the orange had gone out of my life. I found Orange Cat three days later, dead on the road, proving what I hadn't wanted to admit that night on the floor. When Orange Cat left, he didn't mean to come back.

The back of Orange Cat's picture was blank. It wasn't the kind that had the date printed on it, but I remembered the day the photo was taken. It was a day in late April last year, the day Lanie brought home her stupid Bentley mouse. Orange Cat and I spent that day discussing the new house rules, amending them to include not eating pet mice. Every time I opened my bedroom door, he went stalking into the back end of the house, sniffing along the crack under Lanie and Natasha's bedroom door, tail flipping madly. Natasha took the photo under the door crack, back before I accidentally broke her camera. Orange Cat's eye and nose were visible peering under the bedroom door, looking for a mousey snack. I wanted him to peek at me like that so bad, I couldn't stand to look at the picture anymore.

I tapped the photo hello, but did not turn it over. While the other kids ate breakfast, I waited at my desk, flipping through my real estate ads. One of the houses looked prettier than the others. It was big, and too dark, maybe green or blue. I wasn't sure because the picture was in black-and-white. I liked it. If we could move into it today, we could own it like the Sun House and paint it yellow.

I thumbed reverently through my notebook, revisiting the older ads, the ones of houses I was sure must have sold by now, because I didn't know how they couldn't—they were so beautiful. Still, I liked to look at them. I liked to imagine me and Natasha and Gray Cat, and maybe even Lanie and her mouse, inside. I liked to picture us having room to spread out, room for Lanie and Natasha to have bedrooms of their own instead of sharing.

My foot was throbbing and the guilt, mingled with the stress of the night before, made me rock in my chair, back and forth at an even rate. Sometimes I had to rock to alleviate the pressure in my head. If I pulled my hair, I would get a sticker taken away and if I lost all my stickers, I wouldn't get today's real estate section from Mr. Raldy's paper. So I rocked instead, back and forth, faster and faster. I began to feel a gentle rhythm inside my brain, keeping pace with the rhythm of the motion of my body. The rocking made it possible for my brain to time out, to quiet. The rocking was peaceful, like the smooth worn surface of the mud mug I would never touch again. It was like putting on my slippers in the morning, like wrapping a warm sweatshirt around me. I felt safe when I was rocking. The rhythm soothed me.

I rocked and hummed for so long that I almost didn't notice Mrs. Paxton standing beside me. At long length, she patted me on the shoulder, jarring me rudely out of my rhythm.

"You're full of energy today," she said uncertainly. "You must be feeling happy."

I didn't have a word for what I was feeling. It was too tangled up with a half-imaginary factory whistle and the pretty house in the real estate section and the facedown photo in the center of my desk.

"I guess," I said gently, patting her in return. "That must be it." She must have believed me, because she beamed.

The morning dragged because it wasn't structured. With Miss Mandy gone and Mr. Raldy half asleep at his desk, nobody knew exactly when they were supposed to do anything. G tried to keep everyone on track with her picture schedule, but mostly the subs just smiled thinly at her and got a craft out of the closet for us to do. We were champs at glue and glitter. We never cooked anymore, and we studied the calendar sporadically, if the sub remembered at all. We hadn't done money in weeks.

I waited till ten, then past ten, then past eleven, but the speech therapist never came. Schedule changes made me anxious, but Miss Mandy used to talk about being flexible, so I took several deep breaths and kept calm. After lunch was the movie, and today the couch was full. This was a major problem, but I determined quickly that there was nothing to be done. Bristol and Robert both crossed their legs till their knees touched, taking up a whole extra spot. I surveyed the sub, but she did not look interested in helping me. Sometimes it just depended on which adult was in the room.

I could tell Mr. Raldy knew what was happening, but he was big on "letting the sub be in charge," which meant he refused to intervene unless the sub asked him to. I tried to sit on the ottoman, which was the only place left that wasn't a folding chair, but it rolled too easy and it didn't have a back to sink into. Finally, I squeezed myself between the sofa and the wall, humming G notes over and over until Bristol and Robert shushed me. Occasionally G popped over the edge of the sofa upside down, grinning at me, but eventually she stopped and I could hear her snoring softly on the sofa.

Mrs. Paxton found me asleep in my hiding place at three and rushed me on my way, book bag slung over my shoulder and banging my back with every step. Natasha waited at the corner to see that I made it safely to Karen before she biked away.

Karen walked up grinning and full of energy, not like this morning. "Hey there, Lovie."

"Hi, Karen."

"How was school?"

"I had to sit behind the couch."

Karen's head tilted at this, and she opened her mouth to speak, but just then, a silver Jeep Liberty pulled up to the corner and Lanie hopped out, waving good-bye to her classmate Casey. A red ribbon waved from Lanie's hand and Bentley squeaked and rattled in his cage. When Lanie saw me, her smile turned off and her forehead wrinkled up. She let a ten-dollar bill—her prize money—wave in front of me before she jammed it in her pocket, in case I was thinking about taking it. She kept the red ribbon in sight, of course.

"Might have been blue if he hadn't been so sleepy," she said pointedly. Then waved, all smiles again, as Casey's car pulled away. My gaze trailed after the shiny silver Jeep, which I knew belonged to just Casey's mother. Her father drove a black Ford pickup. I wasn't sure how a family could ever get to the point where each parent had their very own car.

"Walking's better anyways," I reassured myself, and noticed Karen's eyes narrow in confusion, then flick from me to the retreating Jeep. Her eye creases got a little deeper.

"Can we celebrate?" Lanie asked, bouncing on her toes and waving the red ribbon high.

"If we stop to leave Bentley at home and pick up Natasha."

I skipped a little at Karen's answer, forgetting my injured foot. Celebrating meant ice cream, if we had the money.

Natasha locked her bike to the stair rail while Lanie took Bentley inside. Then we started toward Probart Street, which was familiar because we had lived on it twice, once in the little white house with black shutters, and once in a trailer at the very far end. Downtown Nabor was three streets over and encompassed four square blocks plus an alley. We walked into it slowly, taking in the unusual warmth of October and the shouts of laughter from a group of teenagers up the street. The empty courthouse was the tallest building in Nabor at two stories high plus a dome, and it sat at the corner of town, facing in. The county seat had long since moved, and the courthouse had stood empty ever since, keeping watch over the smaller buildings, frowning down at all of us.

Karen stretched her arms out and danced, drawing a giggle from Lanie and soft embarrassment from Natasha. I put out my arms, too, and danced in just the same way. A breeze too warm to belong to this month picked my growing hair up off my neck and made goose bumps pop up along my arms. The digital clock at the hardware store turned over from temperature to time with a soft clatter. It was old-fashioned like the store itself, and I loved how its black squares turned over in unison to reveal green, spelling out the things it wanted to tell us. New signs could tell us in pictures and high-color graphics, but I preferred the old way with its soft, familiar sound.

"Good evening, Nabor!" Karen laughed, spinning with her arms out like a child.

"Good evening, Nabor!" Lanie echoed. She was spinning her second-place science fair ribbon around her head like a streamer, and I watched the red satin catch the weak sunlight and sparkle.

Walking through Nabor didn't take much thought.

Once you'd bid farewell to the empty courthouse and stopped to nod hello to Mr. Biamonte at the hardware store, the only thing left to see for two blocks was empty storefronts. The stores were full in the very back of my memory, one stocked with fresh loaves of bread and boxes of macaroni and cheese, the next with shiny gold watches and silver rings, the next with clocks. Nothing in my memory could tell me what had happened to the items now gone from the shelves. They, like the factory, were gone overnight and it seemed the dust was almost immediate, pale on the windowsills, gathering like twilight. The movie theater closed so quick the popcorn boxes remained on the counter, though the popcorn itself had long since been eaten by little gray Bentleys and other furry guests.

It was not terribly uncommon to find buildings empty in Nabor-with-an-A. Since the paper mill stopped blowing its whistle—in theory, anyway—a decade ago, more and more people had made the move to Neighbor and beyond. I think the only reason we didn't move was because of me and my attachment to Nabor, to the familiar streets and the familiar school and the way the town recognized my face. They knew to turn away when I started having a tantrum and they knew who to call if they saw me wandering or lost. It was hard to start fresh with a new group of neighbors when your daughter was a kid like me.

The end of town was marked by U-Save with its single gas pump and its neon orange window molding. My feet knew every scuff in the U-Save's tile, and many of the scuffs, especially the ones in front of the newspaper stand, belonged to me. Though most of the real estate catalogs were from Neighbor-with-an-E, many included a small—and constantly shrinking—selection of homes for sale in Nabor-with-an-A.

"We can't afford magazines today," Karen said, not apologetically but a little guarded, like she hoped I would stay calm. I rolled my shoulders but forced out a breath and didn't answer. The free ones were just as good, anyway, mostly. I took two of these and stuck them in my book bag.

"Livvie took the free ones, just the free ones," I called, casting a sideways glance at the young cashier. I didn't want him to think I was stealing. He eyed me strangely and I ducked my chin to my chest and rolled my shoulders again, willing him to look away. Natasha distracted me with an arm looped through mine and a hand tugging at my ice cream wrapper.

"Need this opened?"

"Yes, please."

We walked back toward Probart Street with our

ice creams, feet picking up quicker as the sun went down. The temperature dropped a degree almost every time the sign above the hardware store switched back, and the goose bumps under my jacket were being replaced with cold patches of red. I licked my ice cream and shivered.

By the time we made it home, half running through the twilight, Lanie had ice cream dripping down her fingers and my hair was stuck in patches to the chocolate on my cheeks. I never remembered I was sticky until after I did things like pet the cat. It was nights like these when I wished we had a working bathtub. The trailer was old and the bathroom had been partially remodeled by someone who had either given up or run out of money before the job was done. The shower worked, but weakly, and the hot water didn't last long. The cracks around the drain meant water went down and spiders came up, both of which made it next to impossible to take a bath. The floor was plywood, although a box of sticky tiles sat in the corner as though waiting for someone to stick them down. Somehow it seemed too permanent a job for my parents to undertake.

Seven minutes into my shower, the water cooled and I emerged unstickied but irritated, wishing I could have soaked my troubles away in a hot bath. I didn't like how the plywood felt on my wet feet and imagined sawdust sticking to me, although it almost never really did. Once in a while I got a splinter in this floor, but usually that was when I kicked and screamed about something.

Picking up a striped towel from the back of the toilet, I scampered down the hall carpet that was flattened by years of other people's feet. In my room, I settled into bed with my two new real estate catalogs. The houses there were all spacious and beautiful. I wasn't sure exactly why I liked them so much, except that I knew the people living in them didn't do things like throw tantrums or drop mugs or fall off chairs in the night. I was pretty sure they didn't hear mysterious whistles, either, but then, I didn't have any way of asking them.

I kept asking Simon and Karen, and sometimes Natasha (but never Lanie) how long it would be before we could buy one of the houses I saw listed in my catalogs. We had lived several different places over the last few years, moving from one house to the next in an attempt to outrun the bills that kept piling up. Shouldn't we just buy a house so we don't have to pay rent? I would ask.

Each family member had their own specific, sad way of answering. Simon liked to ruffle my hair as if I wasn't fourteen years old. He would kiss my cheek and say something like "That's my girl, using that logic." Then change the subject to school or my cat or my real estate catalog. Karen would look away and the crinkles by her eyes would get deeper. She would say something like "Someday, Livvie. Someday we'll stop moving." She always sounded so serious that I didn't even like to ask her anymore. It was like I had brought up something that I wasn't supposed to talk about.

I liked Natasha's answer best, because she didn't let it get her down. "I'm going to tickle you if you ask me that again," she would say, and then she would pin me down and tickle me until I had the hiccups. Natasha's answers were the funniest but also the least informative.

But it was the one person I never asked who had finally answered this question for me. Fixing me with a nasty stare one night at dinner, upset because my classifieds had flopped over into her rice, Lanie informed me coolly, "It's your fault, you know. You're the reason we can't afford to buy that house you're always shopping for."

Natasha slapped her and they both got sent from the table, but not before I understood the way of things. Just like Natasha and Lanie sharing a bedroom, just like Orange Cat and the crinkles by my mother's eyes, our living situation was my fault. I kept getting us into trouble with landlords and neighbors—throwing tantrums, putting dents in the drywall—and we could never settle anywhere long enough to raise the money for a house.

Smoothing down a corner of cool gray newsprint, enjoying the sensation of ink smudging onto my fingers, I was not exactly upset, but urgent with the idea that I needed to fix things.

Chapter 4

I was sitting on the floor coloring a white house yellow with my highlighter when the whistle blew at ten till midnight. Before it even had a chance to fade, I flung myself down the hall and into Natasha's room.

"You heard it, too, right?" I demanded, tossing myself onto her bed. "Did you hear it, Tash?"

Natasha blinked at me drowsily and tugged her book out from under me, stuffing a bookmark in it before she tossed it to the floor.

"Heard what, doodlebug?" she asked with a yawn.

My stomach felt full of pressure all of a sudden.

"You mean you didn't?"

"Didn't what?"

I clenched my shoulders, then my elbows, then my wrists, but it wasn't helping. "Nobody keeps hearing the whistle except for me!" I shouted. "Why can't anybody hear it? Livvie, why are you hearing that whistle? It's not real! You're so stupid, Livvie!"

"No kidding, Livvie! Now shut up!" the lump in the blankets that was Lanie hollered at me.

"Lanie, hush!" Natasha tapped my chin. "Look at me," she said in a commanding voice.

"What?" I did look at her and felt a little of the pressure leak away.

"Stop talking to Livvie like that. She's my sister and I don't like to hear it."

"But—"

"No buts." Stroking back a piece of my hair, she sighed sleepily. "If you're hearing something, then you're hearing something. Maybe I only heard it last time 'cause I was asleep." She leaned closer to my ear. "And don't tell Mom and Dad, but I haven't gone to sleep yet tonight. This is a really flippin' good book." She held it up, but it just looked thick and boring.

"But if you have to be asleep to hear it, doesn't that mean that you're dreaming it?" I ventured.

"It doesn't have to. It could just mean it's something you have to be in a—in a certain state of mind to hear. You know it was ten years ago yesterday that the mill closed down, don't you?"

"Mm-hmm," I said absently.

"Of course you do," she said with a smile. "I should have known you did, you're so good with calendars."

"But I didn't hear it in my sleep. I've been awake both times."

"But you're always in a different state of mind." She didn't say it mean, but it made me clench a little, anyway. "I don't mean that in a bad way," she added quickly. "I just mean you see things different. Not bad. Just different. Maybe you hear them different, too."

I shook my head. "You sound silly," I said, but I no longer felt like I was going to pull my hair. Natasha patted the pillow next to her and I stretched out, starting to feel sleepy.

"Read to me," I murmured hopefully.

"It's too late, hon," Natasha answered. "We both need to get some sleep."

"We all *three* need to get some sleep!" Lanie said loudly from the next bed.

Natasha placed a finger over her lips at me, then flung her pillow as hard as she could at Lanie, who sputtered in protest.

"Hey!"

"Hey!" Natasha mimicked. "I said, stop bad-mouthing Livvie! Now, that goes for both of you!" She tugged my ear and plunked the remaining pillow over my head. Giggling, I pulled my head out and plopped it on top of the pillow instead. Lanie rolled over and hid her own head under her pillow, making a grumpy noise as she did.

Halfway through the night, Lanie got too noisy with her snoring and I had to slip back to my own bedroom. I was half comforted by what Natasha had said, but I still had chill bumps down the back of my neck when I thought about the mill whistle. Back when I was little, Simon and Karen had both worked there and we had owned our Sun House. After the whistle stopped blowing, all the rest of it fell apart. The house. The sun. And Lanie was born, of course, which proved to be an unhappy fact later on.

My foot ached a little as I slipped back into bed, so I logically figured investigating could wait until tomorrow night instead. There was no point in getting in trouble yet by sneaking out at night, not when I would be limping so slow that I probably wouldn't even make it to the mill. But my feet itched toward the door; my eyes kept roaming in that direction. If the mill whistle were something you had to be in a specific frame of mind to hear, well, I wanted to know why I could hear it. Why it was talking to me.

I tossed sideways the other way and pulled my

pillow over my head. No one had put my blankets on, so they were tangled and not lined up properly. From the light outside, it seemed like four a.m., which meant I had almost two hours before I was supposed to be up.

Two hours. Two hours was a long time. Enough time to watch a movie and the beginning of another. Enough time to sleep and dream at least three dreams about Orange Cat, or the Sun House, or perhaps giraffes walking on tightropes. I thought of G and smiled, picturing her in bed right now, bouncing a little in her sleep, dreaming of a smiling giraffe teetering high above the circus tent floor.

But I was not G. I was Livvie Owen and as Livvie Owen, I had a job to do besides dreaming about the circus.

I really needed to know why the mill was calling only me. What it wanted.

The first blanket was the hardest to peel off, because my arms were trapped underneath. Wriggling one loose, I peeled back the soft quilt, then the fleecy blanket underneath, then the woven white blanket I loved best but kept in the middle so it would stay clean. One by one, I peeled my nine tangled blankets off, until I was shivering and barefoot in the four a.m. darkness.

Climbing from the bed carefully, wary of putting

weight on my still-bandaged foot, I stood uncertainly for a moment, shivering with the loss of my blankets. I was going outside, so I ought to wear shoes and jeans and a jacket. Only it was four a.m., which was when I was supposed to wear slippers and pajamas. The clock finally won, aided by the fact that my cold feet ached for fuzzy slippers. It would be almost like bringing bed with me out into the world.

It was cold outside, and almost too dark to be four a.m. My mind conjured up dark smoke, like from a factory, but I knew that really it was only clouds casting such shadows on the night.

I tiptoed the lightest past Lanie and Natasha's window. You couldn't wake Natasha, not for anything, once she was asleep, but if she had woken to read again . . . and then there was Lanie, who seemed to spring awake at the slightest little sound. I wondered again why my sisters and their sleep habits could not have been reversed, the one who loved me waking to help me and the one who hated me sleeping through my noises.

Night dampness seeped into my skin and the pressure inside got bigger. I was tempted to hum, but a hum from the driveway would almost certainly summon a parent or a sister, so instead I hummed in a whisper. It wasn't the same, but it was something.

Anyway, I told myself, I needed to keep my ears clear and sharp, in case the whistle blew.

It never took more than twenty minutes to walk from anywhere to anywhere in Nabor-with-an-A. We had lived so many different places in Nabor that I knew nearly every street, knew the best side to walk on if you wanted room away from cars, knew which houses had dogs and which houses didn't like children.

So it should be easy to walk to the factory, I thought, tugging my sweatshirt tighter around my shoulders. Drafts were working their way in from the back of my slippers and I really wished I had decided to wear shoes instead. It seemed maybe I had been wrong about which outfit was appropriate, but here I was outside and it was too late to go back.

My first job was to sneak through the trailer park. The park was slapped on the side of a hill and Simon sometimes joked that the whole thing would slip to the bottom if it rained too hard. This was our second time living in the trailer park. The first time, I was five and too little to walk down the steep hill by myself without falling. Those were different times.

I crept down the hill past sleeping trailers, long and still, looking smaller when they were sleeping.

The pink lace curtains in only one window showed a light on behind them, and a tall silhouette moved inside. *Neighbor-with-an-E,* I thought. He couldn't work locally if he was up for work already. Nabor-with-an-A didn't open till eight.

My feet didn't know the first block out of the trailer park as well as they knew other parts of Nabor. The next-closest place I'd lived was almost a block and a half away, and quite a few years ago. I remembered Lanie not hating me yet. I remembered we didn't have Orange Cat and that Gray Cat was only a kitten.

The house was small, but it was a house. White with black shutters that didn't serve a purpose, since they didn't actually shut. There were bikes out front now, too few and too new to belong to my family. I always drew the letters of my name on the wall I loved the most, so at this house, I'd left *Livvie Owen Lived Here* on the big back porch that looked tempting in the night. I thought the house winked at me as I passed, and I waved softly.

The street between this and the next place I'd lived was as familiar as Simon's hands or the hallway in my school. The next was an apartment, standing forlornly in a corner of an old building that was once a post office. I was much younger when we lived at this house. There was a wall in the kitchen that was warm with sunshine, and this was where I'd drawn my sentence, each curve and loop of *Livvie Owen Lived Here* sketched from memory of a time someone had shown me the letters and told me what they meant. I couldn't remember who or why. What I remembered about this building was a water fountain in the kitchen and a mail slot between mine and my sisters' rooms. I remembered fluorescent lights that dimmed and brightened willy-nilly, and the way it made me hum a lot more. The memories were distant, as though I were dreaming and tomorrow G could tell me about it with the thought bubble picture on her Velcro strip. But the memory was warm, like fuzzy slippers or nine blankets.

"I think I liked you a lot," I whispered to the apartment building. I was fourteen, so of course I knew apartment buildings couldn't whisper back, but I thought maybe it waved at me a little, just with its curtains. I gave it a wave and a soft, sad smile. It wasn't a sad place, but memories felt that way anyhow.

At the crossroads, I looked longingly left, toward the blue-and-white trailer with my name sketched on the door of the hall closet, toward the cabin with its rough walls and my name drawn on the bathroom windowsill.

Then turned right onto Pendleton Street.

There was longing on this road, too, but it was different. Older and less peaceful. It felt like a scratch that never closed up no matter how many Band-Aids my parents tried to slap on it. This road, it hurt to learn, didn't recall my step. It would have been easier to walk on the other side, where there was less gravel. If I had known in time, I could have crossed at the corner. It wasn't like there were cars at this hour, stealing through the darkness like a burglar, or like me.

"But I didn't know," I said out loud. "I guess I did forget something."

We stopped coming here once the whistle stopped blowing. When we lost our house at the end of the road, when we moved into the trailer park and started the string of rentals we had lived in ever since, none of us quite had the heart to turn right onto Pendleton Street anymore.

Still, as the lawns with their political signs and their plastic riding toys and their mailboxes gave way to vacant lots, to weeds and old beer cans and the start of the fence that would run alongside the factory all the way to the entrance, I felt a familiar feeling whirl up through my stomach and come to rest in my heart.

It wasn't sun yellow anymore, but there it was. The railroad track snaking behind it, the factory holding its hand on the right. It was slightly bigger than the other houses on the street—not big in a fancy way but like it was simply overgrown, too big to be as fanciful as it was, a lot like me. I loved the way it looked at me like it remembered, windows familiar even though the paint had changed from sun yellow to moon white. I loved the way it still smelled of new paper and fried potatoes.

In the dark and the cold, I felt warm, conjuring memories of the gas furnace in the living room, the first place I ever drew my name. You lit it with a switch on top—Karen never let me touch that part—and it made clicking noises. Once it was lit, the fire sprang up inside. I was little, but I knew about fire, so I thought it remarkable that a fire could sit politely in a box on the wall and not burn down the house. The first few times you lit the heat in winter, you smelled gas throughout the house, a smell that always made Karen and Simon nervous, but to Natasha and me, it smelled like warm kitchens and fleece blankets. We stood together in front of the box of flames, arms outstretched with our blankets dripping off the backs of them, capturing the heat together. But even when we weren't there to catch the warmth, the house held it for us, no cracks or gaps for the heat to escape.

This house got a real wave. There was nothing shy about it.

I stood beside the sign tacked to the porch rail and looked at my old bedroom window, all the way on my left, the house's right, beside the factory fence. The window was acting weird, though. Instead of having warmth behind it, it felt cold and distant like it was staring at me, like maybe just this one window didn't recognize me now. Something about the windowpane made me worried, and I clenched and unclenched my shoulders a few times, then started walking a little faster toward the factory.

As I stepped through the gate, hobbling a little on my sore foot that was making me wish I hadn't walked so far, it occurred to me that I really didn't actually have much of a plan. Sometimes I thought ideas and plans were the same thing, and it turned out they were different and now it was too late, almost five according to the light. I was pretty sure the light was accurate, because the clouds had finally started to thin and drift their separate ways.

That's why it scared me so much when it started to rain, and I made a squeaking sound like Bentley and looked straight up into the sky.

Fat raindrops plopped onto my face and one

had the nerve to go straight into my eye. The rest hammered into the soft dirt at my feet, making it sticky. I knew now that I had made the wrong choice. Slippers were not for rain. Slippers were for inside only; there was that rule I had forgotten. Now my slippers would be wet and so would my sleep clothes.

I had really messed up this time.

I started to run, covering my head with my hands like I saw people do in movies. I knew it was silly because a hand is nowhere near as effective as an umbrella. I got mad at myself even for trying, but my hands didn't listen and stayed in the air. My slippered feet shuffled and tripped on the slick, wet dirt and I could feel wet blades of grass tickling up into the back of my slippers. It made me feel like I had swallowed something slimy.

"This was a stupid idea, Olivia!" I shouted as I ran for cover under the nearest roof I saw. My hand dropped from my head to cover Orange Cat's collar in my pocket, hoping I could manage to keep it dry. Cats didn't like wet. "You do not have very good ideas sometimes, young lady! Slippers are not for rain! They are to stay inside! Don't you dare go outside in your slippers, Livvie Owen!"

My voice cranked up a little louder, but the roof I had found was empty and no one would hear. It was the oddest thing, my roof. It was standing by itself on stilts, with no walls. It seemed to be there solely to protect a bench.

The bench stirred something in the back of my memory and I shivered hard and did not sit, even though my foot was throbbing and my slippers were soggy. The night air cold but familiar on my face, I thought maybe I remembered this bench.

I smelled the paper. That was the strongest part, once the memory took hold. Somehow after all these years, the paper mill smell never quite faded from the streets and the trees and the sidewalks of Nabor, but back then it was different. More solid. Everyone hated it, talked about how awful it smelled, but to me it smelled like home.

We sat on the bench—all four of us, and that was the whole family then, although from the look of Karen, that was going to change soon—while we waited for the bus, back when there was a reason for Neighbor's bus to run to Nabor. When the bus came, a big, smelly contraption blowing smoke and darkness all over the sky and scaring me with its round, staring headlights, Natasha grabbed my hand on one side and Karen on the other and we all climbed aboard.

"Don't, don't, don't," I said to Karen. I wasn't very good at words back then, usually using the same one over again instead of finding a second or a third. "Livvie, don't."

"You're okay, Livvie-bug," Karen said. "We're going to the city, that's all."

It was the simplest, briefest memory, but it felt so warm and so familiar that I wanted to crawl under it like a blanket. Inching my wet self down onto the bench, I shivered in the darkness that was getting darker as the clouds came back. *Here I am,* I thought. *At the factory. Whistle if you dare.* But the whistle remained stubbornly silent and I realized, now that I was here, that I hadn't the first clue which building the whistle sounded from.

Funny thing about being Livvie Owen. Sometimes the more difficult thoughts, the ones like "I know the way to the paper mill, I might as well walk it," occurred to me long before the simple ones. Here in the darkness, for the first time, it occurred to me that for a whistle to blow, a button had to be pushed or a chain pulled.

That meant a hand, which belonged to a person.

Tighter and tighter down into the bench I pressed myself. Closer and closer the dark pressed in around. Pressure started to build in my chest, in my stomach. Pressure and fear as I started to rock gently. My hands found their way into my hair and began to tug.

"This was a stupid idea, Livvie Owen," I whispered. "Don't you dare leave the house alone, young lady."

Another thing, though, about being Livvie Owen. She rarely ever listened when I spoke to her. Usually when she did, it was already too late.

I rocked and tugged until the rain began to lessen, till the clouds began to go their separate ways. The shaggy fabric of my slippers was clumped together from the wet, and the backs of the slipper heels were muddy. My own heels were muddy and the feeling was cold and yuck and slime. My skin felt crawly, my muscles clenching over and over as I tried to release the pressure.

I wanted to go home, but walking here was such a bad idea that I did not want to walk anymore. "I've learned," I said out loud. Miss Mandy was always telling me to stop and take stock of what I'd learned, and, once in a long while, I thought to obey. "I've learned something today." Sitting firmly on the bench as the rain blew away and the light started to come, I remained planted like the trees overgrowing themselves along the fence line. My fists rolled up, pinkies wrapping around my ring fingers, thumbs pressing on my middle knuckles. I pressed my thumb knuckles into the spaces behind my ears so my hum got louder inside my head. "Hmmmm. Hmmmm."

Furious G notes, one after another. If I could stop the pressure, I could get this situation under control. If I sat long enough, someone would come and get me, like the bus that day. They were going to have to do it. I simply could not do it for myself.

Chapter 5

Orange Cat found me one day when I was lost in Walmart, and that was how he joined us. He was chasing a moth, quite unconcerned, through the lawn and garden section when I saw him, and the minute I did, I knew he was for me. He was only a little scrap of a thing then, and so tiny it was almost difficult to imagine him getting as fat as he later would. He was striped and his baby kitty belly was tight and bloated with worms. His meow sounded like sandpaper on rusty metal. I picked him up that first day, his stubby little legs sticking out in all directions, and he immediately bumped his face against me to claim me. Somehow, with Orange Cat cuddled up under my chin, his baby claws kneading, I was able to focus and find my way back to the toy department.

The entire three years Orange Cat was in my life, I felt calmer and happier than I ever did before and certainly since. Touching him was like touching my mud mug or sliding my feet into my slippers. He was pure comfort, like my nine blankets or my real estate book. He also happened to be my best friend.

The little collar around my wrist, his very first, was all I had left of him and I rubbed it and rubbed it, but it didn't feel the same as petting him. I sat on the bench while the sun came up, and by then the sky thought the rain had never been. Maroon and dark purple worked up from the horizon first, followed by streaks of ice blue that shattered the blackness all the way up to the stars.

"Dumb stars," I said to no one. "Where were you three hours ago?"

I figured it had to be seven by now. It almost never got light until we were all piled in the car, on our way to school, and that was right about seven. My slippers were still soggy and I could tell they were going to dry stiff. They would never feel right on my feet after this.

Some time ago, I had become aware of my hands. They were, quite on their own, acting out a finger play I didn't remember. Something about a church and a steeple, I thought, but I couldn't be certain. I had never been good at charades, although my hands apparently thought otherwise.

From the bench, I could just make out the world beyond the factory gate. Lights were beginning to spring on in houses. Cars were beginning to chase each other, out on the main road. Headlights dimming as the sky grew brighter. Windows catching the glint of the sun.

The factory whistle, apparently, was not something that wanted to be chased or caught. Six o'clock had come and gone and I hadn't heard so much as a single note. My feet crossed and uncrossed. My hands continued their play, over and over, fingers tepeed like a building, then flipping to interlace like the people inside. I had never really understood the point of such games. I think maybe it was something I'd seen Natasha do once, but I hadn't the faintest clue when.

I was calmer now and thought I could probably walk home, but I'd been sitting for so long that I wasn't sure whether I should change my game now. If I planned on walking home, I should have done it three hours ago, when the world was still dark. It was light now. It was day. What if I walked on a different street than the one Karen and Simon used when they came looking for me? What if I got turned around and only *thought* that I knew the way home?

Every five minutes I sat, I was five minutes closer to my family coming to find me. I was afraid by standing I would restart some kind of cosmic timer, so I stayed seated even as the wind picked up, even as the school day started without me.

And sure enough, not five minutes later, I saw the first headlights of the day arc off the main road onto Pendleton Street, bumping their way across the potholes to the factory gate.

Still, I didn't stand. My eyes roamed to the trees leaning gracefully over the fence toward the Sun House. There was something to be said for putting down roots. I was a girl with a tentative grasp on emotions and there was no telling which ones Simon and Karen would be experiencing this morning. Beginning to rock, just slightly, I kept my humming to a minimum, just barely this side of under my breath. The car took shape and became definitely ours, which was a relief in spite of my concerns.

They must not have seen me right away, because the car stopped just shy of the factory gates and wavered toward the Sun House like it was going to turn in. It was not the same car we'd had back then. Our car back then had been a Nova and we lost it for a while. Three cars later, it was a red Toyota Tercel that finally laid its headlights across me and, that mystery solved, began bouncing once again in my direction.

I stretched out one leg and my knee crackled at the change of positions. A little more carefully, I followed with the other leg. The Tercel picked up speed, then shimmied in the mud and slid to an ungraceful stop by my bench. Doors were flung open and feet hit the ground. And *still* I didn't stand.

"You've done it now, Livvie Owen," I whispered, careful to keep this, like the humming, just under the surface of a whisper. "You've caused quite the uproar now, young lady."

I needn't have whispered, because no one could have heard me over my father's strong voice shouting, "Olivia!"

And my mother right behind him, still in her slippers, with her hair down on her shoulders. She must have been as confused as I was about what was okay to wear out of the house, and when. "Livvie? Are you all right?"

They were both shouting and I wasn't sure when I should answer, because they both kept asking. Simon swept me up off the bench, standing me on my sleeping feet so quickly I almost toppled over. I couldn't have fallen, though, not with his arms tight around me. "Are you all right? Are you all right?"

Over and over so quick it made my ears dizzy. I didn't have language all of a sudden. I could have made use of a Velcro strip like G's.

"Livvie, what were you thinking?" This was Karen, more sensible than Simon. She assessed me quickly with her eyes and figured out I was okay. "When we woke up and you were gone—Livvie—what did you think you were doing?"

This question, so much more interesting than a simple "Are you all right," stopped Simon silent and he, too, stepped back to look at me. His warm hands stayed on my forearms and I let him hold me up.

"I—"

That one word, all alone, came back, so I said it two or three more times.

"I—I—"

"Let's—" Simon said at the same time, talking over my "I"s. "Let's get her in the car. It's freezing out here."

Between them, as if I might escape again if they gave me an opening, they led me to the car. The inside of the Tercel was warm and I worried about my wet clothes soaking up the seat, but I didn't have the words yet to explain.

Karen guided me into the backseat and slid in beside me. "Don't worry about the water," she said in a voice higher than her usual one, like she couldn't believe I would hesitate about something as silly as the car's upholstery. Karen was like that. She understood without understanding. Knew what I was worried about, but not why.

Simon was more of a "why" kind of guy, so it was him I fixed my gaze on as my language finally started to come back.

"I heard the factory whistle at eleven-forty-eight last night, and I wanted to investigate."

Karen's hands found my face. "Tell me you haven't been here since eleven—"

"I went to Natasha first. I slept in there for a while. But when I woke up because Lanie was snoring so loud, and I went back to my room, I wanted to—I wanted to know. Because Natasha said maybe you have to be in a certain state of mind to hear the whistle and if it's only whistling for people in a state of mind like mine, I want to know how come." There were too many feelings all tangled up in my head for me to make sense of one or to settle on something. Karen stayed stiff, holding me at arm's length as Simon put the car in reverse. We bumped and sputtered across the weeds and the ruts of the factory road, long unused by anyone but us.

"Olivia, what would possess you?" Karen pleaded. The crinkles around her eyes got deeper and then something horrible happened, something I couldn't remember happening for a long time. Karen's eyes started shining extra bright as if there was water forming in them.

I reached out one cold hand, finally shaken loose from its absurd finger play, and stroked it down my mother's cheek.

"I made you cry," I observed. "I didn't want to do that, Mom."

Her stiff arms folded into soft Mom ones, and she drew me tight into her embrace.

We were almost back across town when the hug finally ended. Drawing back, she looked me in the eye and I was relieved to find hers dry.

"We'll talk more later," she said. "You need to go to bed for a while."

I blinked twice. "But it's a school day."

"Honey, you've been out all night and you're a mess. Let me get you cleaned up and you can catch up on some sleep."

"But it's—but it's a school day." A weird sort of panic started trailing up from my stomach to settle in my throat. "I'm not supposed to stay home from school unless I'm sick. That's called skipping."

"Livvie, honey, you're too tired for school. Sometimes that's the same thing as being sick."

Now tears started forming in my own eyes and I drew my knees up to my chest. "I never meant to do something serious enough to stay home from school. I only wanted the whistle to stop. I only—I—Karen, I didn't mean to. Just let me go to school."

"Liv—"

"Please, just let me go to school. I'll be okay."

"Livvie, honey—"

"Okay, I'm going. That's all. I have to go to school and fix this."

"Olivia." It was the first time my father had spoken since the paper mill, and his voice had changed from the worried tone he'd used there to a tone I hadn't heard him use in years. The anger in his voice made my own voice silence quickly. "Go to bed," he said, quieter, as he put the car in park.

I nodded tensely and opened the passenger door. Karen followed me out, but Simon stayed behind the wheel.

"Isn't Simon coming?" I asked my mother.

"He's got to drive your sisters to school." Her tone was still funny, but her arm slipped around my shoulders as she led me to the door.

Lanie met me on the steps, hair swept up into an elaborate set of braids, purple sweatshirt almost looking new from her embroidery. She flung her arms around me at the door and squeezed me tight, then stepped back and frowned at me fiercely.

"Geez, Liv. Do you know how bad I was going to

feel if I called you stupid and then you ran off and died like Orange Cat?"

The excitement of the night, coupled with Lanie's odd behavior and the mention of Orange Cat, was simply too much. Standing on the wooden step with one hand on the storm door, I started to cry. And that, like everything else, was something I just couldn't do the way you were supposed to. Great whooping sobs came bursting out of nowhere and I grabbed Lanie around the neck and held her tight.

"God, calm down. Jeez." She sounded scornful and slightly disgusted, much more like herself than she had a moment ago, but her hand wound around and patted me awkwardly. I sniffled and got ahold of myself, peeling myself off Lanie's shoulder. She straightened her purple sweatshirt and wrinkled her nose at me.

"Mom, I think she got snot on my shoulder," she hollered.

Karen was spared answering by Simon's sudden short blast on the car horn. I looked down at him. From up here on the steps, he looked different. Too big for the small car he drove. Too angry to be *my* Simon.

"Lanie, we'd better get going." This from Natasha, who came rocketing out the door and down the stairs, edging sideways between me and Lanie. "Dad doesn't look too happy to be waiting, and having to drive us to school on top of it—well—I just don't think we'd better make him wait much longer, that's all."

Bewildered, I watched Natasha land at the bottom of the stairs, having taken a flying leap off the second step up. Mom's hand tightened on my damp elbow for a second. I wasn't sure what I had expected, but I knew Natasha ignoring me was just as out of character as Lanie hugging me, no matter where I had been that night.

"Hey, Natasha . . ." I said uncertainly, but there was still something wrong with my voice, and it wasn't loud enough for Natasha to hear me over the car's running engine and Lanie's prattle about her ruined sweatshirt.

"Come on, Livvie," Mom said, firmly guiding me by the shoulders into the house. "Let's get you warm and in bed."

"But Tash . . ." My voice trailed off as my hand trailed behind me, pointing backward at the Tercel disappearing down the hill. My arm suddenly felt very tired and I let it fall limply at my side.

Karen looked at me with something I think was called sympathy. "She'll be all right. You just scared her, Livvie." Eyes casting away from mine, crinkles getting deeper again by half. "You scared us all. Lord God."

I started to cry again, gentler this time but no less sudden. "I'm sorry. . . ."

Karen let out this long, shaky sigh and pulled me into a tight hug, the very best kind.

"Oh, hush," she said quickly. "You're all right."

But I didn't feel all right.

"I feel like an idiot with a capital whatever *idiot* starts with," I murmured into her sleeve.

"Iiiiii . . ." She drew out the sound. "What letter do you hear?"

I drew back from her shoulder and put my hands on my hips like I had seen Lanie do a million times. "Do I look like I'm in the mood for phonics?"

My mother threw her head back and laughed an amazed sort of laugh. She placed a firm hand on my back and guided me through the door. "All right, fine," she said. "Forget I asked."

With weak water pressure, I wasn't inspired to stay in the shower for long. Soon, I fell into bed, tucked in under nine warm blankets with my fish lamp swirling and a quilt over the window to keep out the sun. My mother fell asleep almost immediately, lying in bed with me with her arm draped over my shoulder. I think she was afraid to leave me alone, in case I would disappear again. She looked younger when she was asleep, and it seemed funny—

funny in a weird way, that is, not the kind that makes you laugh—to see her that way.

I was glad she was able to sleep. At least somebody could. It was all I could do even to lie still and stay in bed. My fingers and toes kept crossing, my shoulders tensing and relaxing, my teeth chewing my lips, a hum just under the surface. There were too many things to figure out, too many memories of my midnight adventure to sort through.

It was difficult to move slowly, as wound up as I was, but if I woke Karen, she would get upset that I was drawing the Sun House. She might think I was planning to run away again. So I moved slowly and carefully as I slid my notebook and pencil off the nightstand. I sketched the house as best I could remember, not as it used to be, not as I had sketched it a million times, but as it looked now. I wasn't much of an artist and my drawings usually looked more like somebody had closed their eyes and attacked a piece of paper with a dirty shoe—at least that's what Lanie always said—but if there was one thing I could draw, it was letters, so I finished the drawing by adding the letters I'd seen on the sign tacked to the porch railing.

Sketching them in further and further detail—first their shapes, then their shades, then the dampness of the cardboard underneath, I imagined what the letters must say. In my heart I knew they said For Rent. They simply *had* to. What else could a sign in front of the Sun House say? It couldn't say For Sale because we had already done that, years ago. But we hadn't rented yet, so surely that was still an option.

Satisfied with my notion to rent the Sun House for my family, I was at last able to drop into a shallow sleep.

Chapter 6

I woke up sick and said into the darkness, "Great going, Livvie, now you've messed up again."

Karen shifted in her sleep and mumbled something about potatoes, making me jump. I had forgotten she was over there.

The light had changed. I could tell even with the quilt over the window that a big chunk of the day had passed while I was asleep with my face on my notebook. Sitting up and wiggling out from under Karen's heavy arm, I rubbed the sleep out of my eyes and blinked around me.

Someone sat so still in my chair, it took me a moment to process.

"Oh," I said at last, feeling a weird emotion I couldn't quite name vibrating through me. I wasn't sure if it was even my own emotion, or if I was see-ing it on Lanie.

"Don't wake Mom" was all she said, in a voice soft as a whisper.

I shook my head and pressed my lips together tightly to show her I had no intention of speaking. Groggy as I was for sleeping the whole day away, and crummy as I was feeling with my throat sore and my head hot and funny, I wasn't sure I would have had the words to speak, anyway.

Lanie stood and motioned for me to follow her to the door. Sliding sideways out from under the covers, I felt automatically for my slippers, and my spirits plummeted when I remembered they were ruined. In the space of two days, I had lost two of my biggest comfort items: my fuzzy slippers and my mud mug. Anxiously, my hands fumbled with the kitten collar on my wrist. I rubbed the worn brass tag like a worry stone.

When I was too slow in following Lanie, she reached out and took my hand. "Come on already," she whispered, a little awkwardly. "We need to talk."

I nodded dumbly again and let her lead me out the door and down the hall to her bedroom. Auto-matically, I checked for Natasha, but she was nowhere in sight.

"She didn't come home from school yet," Lanie said. "She said she had a study group."

Lanie sat me on Natasha's bed and, when I made no move to do so for myself, pulled the quilt up around my shoulders. Then she crossed the room to settle on her own neatly smoothed quilt, pulling her jeaned leg up to her chin the same way I did. Beside her on the bed was a plate with half a sandwich and some Dorito crumbs. She munched absently while she studied me.

"You have a fever," she said after a minute, somewhat accusingly.

"I didn't mean to," I answered, tucking myself tighter down into Natasha's blanket.

Lanie rolled her eyes. "I didn't say you did. I'm just saying . . . You have a fever and if Mom and Dad see me talking to you, they'll think I'm teasing you, so I wanted to catch you before Mom woke up."

I rocked a little, confused at her odd behavior, and my hands, all alone, began their odd finger play again. "What do you want to talk about? What do you want to talk about?" My words got jumbled up in nerves and came out twice.

"Liv, you really scared me last night. And then I talked to my teacher today and she really scared me, too. She said if you ran off and something had happened to you, I would have felt really bad for being so mean to you all the time. She said—" Lanie stopped and stared out the window for a second. I followed her gaze and found a setting sun and an orange October sky. Almost a whole day had passed without my knowledge. I felt uneasy. Lanie cleared her throat and drew my gaze again.

"My teacher talks a lot and I don't always understand," I prompted, thinking maybe Lanie's problem was that she was confused by what her teacher had said and didn't know how to retell it. This was a problem I understood well.

But Lanie shook her head. "I understood," she said flatly. "Too well. I just—I wanted to call a truce. That's all. Do you know what a truce is?"

"Like a peace agreement. Like at the end of the war."

She looked at me a little surprised. "Yeah. Like that."

"You want to call a peace agreement?"

"I want to stop fighting unless you really do something to deserve it."

I smiled a little at her and she smiled uncertainly back. She was funny. This time in a laughing way.

"Okay, Lanie," I said. "We can have a peace agreement. Can I go do my catalogs now?"

"Who's stopping you?" Lanie turned away as if

she had never been staring at me in the first place. "Don't wake Mom, though."

"I won't." I made it halfway to the door, still dragging Natasha's quilt. "Where's Simon?"

"He stayed out. He had to pick up Natasha."

I was almost out the door when Lanie started talking again.

"If you do anything like that again, I won't call a truce. I'll declare war. Okay?" She looked away and her face crinkled up like it pained her to admit it. "You really scared me, jerk."

"Me, too."

In the bedroom, I found that Mom had rolled over and hid her face in my pillow. I sat on the edge of the bed and watched her sleep for a few moments. Her breathing was so slow and soft. In and out. In and out. I wondered if this was what I looked like when I was sleeping. Mom would know, because she watched me sometimes. I thought about waking her to ask her, but I was pretty sure Lanie would get mad at me if I did it.

And maybe for another reason, too, I let Mom sleep. When she was sleeping, the crinkles by her eyes were softer and not nearly so deep. An absurd thought struck me and I wondered if Mom looked so stressed out and tired when she was talking to people other than me.

Gray Cat stole out from beneath the covers, looking guilty at being caught sleeping next to a warm body other than mine. I sat back and let her pick her way up onto my lap, where she placed a pink paw pad on my shoulder. Looking me in the eye, she bumped her cold nose against my chin and made a squeaky sound.

"I love you, Gray Cat," I said, suddenly worried I hadn't told her this enough of late. Saying "I love you" to any cat was hard when there wasn't any orange in the picture, but it wasn't Gray Cat's fault. She was a good cat and I did love her, just differently than I had loved my overweight orange kitty.

The way Gray Cat looked at me without blinking for a minute, I knew she understood what I had said and also why I hadn't said it for such a long time. Bumping her face against mine a little harder this time, she rubbed her whiskers along my cheekbone. Claiming me, Natasha had explained once, back when she wasn't mad at me.

Mom woke at seven and immediately began trying to get me to take cough syrup even though I didn't have a cough.

"If they intended it for people who didn't have a cough, they would have called it 'non-cough syrup,'" I explained in what I was certain was a patient voice for the four hundred and forty-seventh time.

90

"They called it 'cough syrup' because it's sup-posed to prevent you from *developing* a cough," she insisted. "You already have a fever and a sore throat. The last thing you need is a cough."

"No, the last thing I need is cough *syrup*," I protested. I could not tolerate the texture of cough syrup. The way it slimed down my throat made me think I was swallowing toads or snake skin. I would rather have the cough.

Karen sighed and relented, slumping into the nearest chair. Her ankles crossed and uncrossed and her fingers tapped on the tabletop. You could blame what you wanted on autism, but if you watched my mother for a minute, you would realize that a lot of my nervous fidgets, I came by honest. Like mother, like daughter.

I was studying my mother, trying to figure out whether she was where my hands had learned the finger play, when my ears picked up the sound of tires on the gravel. Running to the door and flinging it open, letting in a blast of October night, I bounced on my toes. At last I could put this uneasiness to rest. My sister and my father had come home and now they would hug me like everything was okay and it would be like I had never made my ill-advised midnight journey.

The car door creaked open into a frosty night too

cold to be October. My sister climbed out first, swinging a heavy book bag over her shoulder and climbing the stairs two at a time, which was more a Lanie trait than a Natasha one. She slipped past me at the door with a quick "Hello." Grabbing the Cheerios box off the top of the fridge, she headed for her room.

As I watched her go, Gray Cat following her like a traitor, I felt a frown crinkling up on my forehead. " 'Hello'?" I mimicked. "Is that all I get?" Humming a G note, I turned to the door again, hoping for a decent greeting from my father.

But he came through even more quickly than my sister, and although he dropped a hand on my shoulder as he passed, he didn't even speak. Since the Cheerios were gone, he took the cornflakes. He was the only person I had ever met who could eat cornflakes with no milk.

Karen sighed shortly and turned off the stove, where water had just begun simmering for macaroni and cheese. She handed me a yogurt, even though she knew I couldn't drink it without my mug.

I wasn't hungry, anyway. The kitchen was so much emptier now than it had been moments ago, when it was warm with anticipation. Natasha's door opened and my breath caught in hope, but it was

Lanie tossing out Gray Cat before she got a chance to eat Bentley. I caught my ears still listening for the car in the drive, because its coming had been so drastically unsatisfying.

"They'll be home any minute," I whispered. "They'll say 'Hey there, Olivia,' and I'll say 'Hey there, Simon, hey there, Tash,' and they'll talk to me for a minute and then Natasha will read me something." Rocking on my toes and humming softly, I stayed in the doorway too long.

"Livvie, come away from the door before Gray Cat notices it's open," Karen said without lifting her eyes from the table. I quickly slammed the door, not wanting a repeat performance of Orange Cat's disappearance. "You don't need to be out in the night air, anyway. You're sick," my mother added, dragging herself out of her chair to cross the room to me. "Come on, Liv. Bedtime."

"But I don't want to go to bed yet. I don't want to go to bed yet."

"I know." She guided me with an arm around my shoulders. "But the rest of the house does, Liv."

"Houses don't go to bed." I giggled.

"You're funny." Mom reached around me to turn off the light over the stove.

"Houses don't go to bed, just people do."

"You know, you're right. And people also *stay* in bed. All night. Without standing on chairs. Without sneaking out to paper mills."

My smile stopped and I looked at Karen tensely. "I know that, I know."

She ruffled my hair, but didn't answer. Somehow, I wasn't convinced that she believed me.

Chapter 7

The minute I stepped inside the house, I knew something was wrong. The gas furnace was missing; all that was left was a broken pipe sticking out of the darkened wall. The carpet under my feet smelled like the last person who had stepped on it lived and died a hundred years ago. The smell was wet and hot, like the time we went camping in the backyard at the trailer and it rained on our campfire and put it out. The walls, once off-white, were gray and beginning to crumble. My ears took in quiet, broken only by dripping water. No hum of electricity coursing through the walls, no creak of a footfall or whisper of a memory.

"We left the Sun House all alone," I said to Orange Cat.

And he really was there at my feet, guiding me through the house. The minute I saw him, I knew I was dreaming and became aware of the blankets touching my skin, of the fish lamp's soft whir near my left ear. Orange Cat's crooked tail twitched once at my thoughts, as though I had broken some rule by realizing it was a dream.

"I'm listening," I whispered to Orange Cat. "Just because I'm dreaming doesn't mean I'm not listening."

Orange Cat squeaked his funny meow, and I followed him into a bedroom where the curtains were once yellow, where the obsession with fish began because of the ocean-themed paper on the walls.

Tonight, there was hardly any paper. What was left was peeling down and down slowly in narrow strips. The windows were curtainless and boarded up, the glass trapped cruelly behind unfriendly lengths of plywood. There were crude moon shapes cut into the plywood, letting me glimpse dark silver moonlight that never truly reached inside.

"What is this?" I asked Orange Cat, reaching down, aching to pick him up and hold him against me. He ducked my hand and trotted to the corner, where a familiar plastic food dish sat empty.

"You're hungry?" I asked him, and he meowed. "You're honestly hungry at a time like this?"

Orange Cat nudged the bowl insistently. I reached to pet him again and he hissed, eyes flashing from *orange to pale yellow. It was suddenly very cold and damp inside the Sun House.*

"Livvie didn't forget," I whispered urgently to Orange Cat. "It's not that I forgot. It's just—kitties don't eat when they're dead."

Orange Cat growled deep in his throat, and I started backing away just as he lunged at me.

"Natasha!"

"Mhmmmph."

"Tash, Livvie had a nightmare!"

Natasha was asleep facedown on top of her book, with only a few pages to go. It must have been a scary book, because she jumped awake when I tapped her again, guarding her face from invisible dangers.

"What—"

Her sleepy eyes blinked twice and then focused. Her hands dropped.

"Olivia?" Her shoulders slumped tiredly. "What are you doing?"

"I had a bad dream," I whispered, crawling insistently under the quilt even though Natasha made no move to invite me.

For a moment, she stayed stiff, holding the quilt tighter so I couldn't quite get covered. Then a long, loud sigh racked her and she relaxed. I inched a little more of the quilt for myself and scooted back against my sister.

"What did you dream?" she asked tiredly in a voice that sounded like Karen's.

"I dreamed about the Sun House. Orange Cat was showing me it, and it was empty and all messed up."

Natasha sighed again, shifted uncomfortably. "We left it pretty messed up, Liv."

"Nuh-uh, it was perfect. But not in my dream, in my dream, it was messed up. Orange Cat showed me his empty food bowl, and he hissed at me like I forgot to—" My voice breaking was unexpected and so were the tears that suddenly flooded my eyes. I could bear the thought of a broken Sun House and I could at last bear the thought of Orange Cat being gone, if only just. But the idea that he was alone in that place and that he thought I had forgotten him . . .

"Oh, Livvie."

"What?" I sniffled, and Natasha chuckled, a deep, soft sound.

"Nothing. I was just saying your name for the fun of it," she said. "Livvie, Livvie."

"Tasha, Tasha," I echoed, and in saying her name, I stopped crying. We lay there like that for several moments in the darkness, having declared not quite a truce, but something similar.

"Your fever broke," Natasha said after a moment, wrapping her arm around so that her hand could reach my forehead.

"I'm good at breaking things," I pointed out, and Natasha laughed a surprised sort of laugh.

"Who isn't, in this house?" she asked wearily.

"Hey, Natasha?"

"Yeah, bug?"

"Is Simon mad at me?"

"You scared Dad really bad, honey. He had his hand on the phone to dial the police when I thought of where you must be. He was terrified for you. And do you know, he was already upset about the house and then you vanished and he thought you'd over-heard him. . . ."

"Upset about what house?"

Natasha shifted to prop herself on her elbow and look at me.

"This one, bug. Didn't you know? We got an-other slip."

My mind quickly flashed back to the broken mug, to the hole in the living room wall, to my screaming. Complaints from neighbors wore on a landlord and then when they came in, when they saw the dents in the drywall . . .

"When?"

"Yesterday."

"So . . ." I calculated quickly. "The third Thursday in November, we have to be out?" The slips were always for thirty days.

"That sounds about right."

"Why didn't anyone tell Livvie?" I asked in a tiny voice.

"I guess they thought maybe you'd run away, or that you would hurt yourself, or that it would give you nightmares, but since you've taken care of all of those already . . ." She sighed a shaky sound.

I began to rock back and forth against her, the hum working its way up from my stomach. My hands were trapped under the blankets and Natasha hugged me tighter, maybe so I couldn't get them free.

"I shouldn't have told you," she said after a minute. "Sometimes I'm not sure what to tell."

Swallowing the hum and forcing my body to stop rocking, blowing hard through pursed lips, I said, "It's okay, Livvie's okay, Livvie's okay."

Natasha looked at me. Her eyes got smaller. "Are you really?"

"I'm okay," I repeated, my mind flashing back to that night in the kitchen, to Janna's anger, to my father's vow to begin looking someplace other than my hometown. A deep breath, my voice coming out only a little higher than normal. "I'm okay."

Natasha walked me back to bed and tucked me in, asking me once more whether I was all right. I hugged her good night and promised I was fine. The minute she was gone, I began to rock so hard the bed shook. *What a mess,* I thought in exhaustion. *What a mess.*

I should have known when I woke up that it was going to be a bad day, because my first words were "Get off me, you lump! I can't breathe!"

Gray Cat complied with a glare that said, *This is MY idea.*

Simon was at the table when I trailed into the kitchen. He sat hunched up, studying the chaotic pages of newsprint scattered on the table in front of him. Lanie tapped him hello on the head, pulled the milk from the fridge, and left the kitchen, still drinking out of the jug. Simon occasionally circled something in red ink. He glanced up when I stopped next to him.

"Hey, doodlebug," he said kindly.

I sat down in the chair beside him and folded my arms on the table. "Does that mean you're finished being mad?"

Simon looked up from his paper briefly, then started circling things again.

"Was never mad," he said. "You just gave an old

man a heart attack when you ran away, that's all." I learned long ago that Simon used silly phrases that didn't mean what they said. Although I hadn't given anybody a heart attack, I had definitely scared him for him to compare it.

"Didn't run away," I protested, using his pattern of speech a little bit by dropping the "I" off the front of my sentence. "Just wanted to find out why the whistle was blowing."

Simon ran a hand down his face, leaving smudges of newsprint.

"Honey, you can't just leave the house alone."

I think my voice might have accidentally raised some. "Livvie knows, Livvie knows that already!"

Simon had less patience than Karen for my raised voice.

"Olivia, don't start that stuff."

"Don't start what?" I demanded. "Olivia, don't you start! Don't you dare—" I broke into a hum and rocked forward and back a few times, evening the pressure in my head. Simon abruptly closed his newspaper.

"I'm going to wake Natasha," he said shortly, and although I was no expert, I thought I might still be hearing anger in his voice.

"Fine, just make him mad, Olivia!" I hollered. "You sure are good at messing things up!" Bolting from the table, I ran back into my bedroom and flung myself at the bed. Gray Cat hissed in protest and skittered out from under the blankets.

Moments later, I felt stupider than ever. I couldn't stay in bed all day, not after I was absent from school yesterday. I would definitely be considered truant for that. But to get out now, I would have to walk right past my father, and it was difficult to walk past someone you had just run away from, slamming the door as you went. I could hear him and Natasha shuffling around in the kitchen. Crouching next to the door, I listened.

When the kitchen fell silent, presumably because everybody in it was busy eating, I drew a deep breath and bolted past them with my book bag banging on my shoulder. I would wait in the car for my mother.

The light faded earlier with every passing day, I thought as I sat in the car. It was cold out and the sun hadn't managed yet to clear the top of the mountain. A little later every day. There was a day in late autumn, a day just like this with the taste and the smell and the thinness of the air just the same, when Orange Cat walked up to me in our yard on Main Street and meowed to be picked up.

I had lifted him and kissed the fuzzy top of his head. I wasn't sure what else to do besides that, but he seemed to really want something. His fur was damp with frost and his paw pads wet when he placed them on my face.

"You aren't supposed to be out here," I said sternly. "Livvie, you had better keep a closer eye on your cat." Orange Cat meowed in protest, but I took him inside, anyway, and left him on my bed with Gray Cat.

Today was so similar, the air the same weight and taste and color, that I felt like I should be able to reach through this day to that day last year and spend another minute with my Orange Cat. Karen's arrival in the car jolted me from this useless hope, and I began to hum frantic G notes.

"Livvie, you're in your pajamas," Karen said. "Hurry in and change."

"I have the right shoes on."

"You don't have the right clothes on."

I surveyed my ratty sweatpants and sweatshirt. "These are, technically, not pajamas."

"I technically don't care what they are. You're not wearing them to school. Please go change."

"I don't want to run into Simon."

"He's your father. You live in the same house. You're going to run into him at some point, anyway, so it might as well be while you're staying out of trouble by doing what I've asked you to do. Quick,

quick. You're going to be late for school and you're going to make your sisters late again."

As if I'm not under enough pressure, I thought. Humming louder, I leapt from the car and dashed back into the house. I ran through the kitchen with my eyes closed, banging into the table and whacking my elbow on the corner of the door frame as I careened down the hallway to my bedroom.

"Livvie, get dressed and hurry!" I bellowed, basically diving into a clean T-shirt and a more-or-less-unwrinkled pair of jeans. "Let's go now!"

Back through the kitchen with my eyes closed, banging into chairs and the edge of the table. I heard a loud sigh, but Simon didn't say anything. I heard him right something plastic that I had knocked over.

Lanie had arrived in the car while I was gone and, wonder of wonders, she had actually left the front seat open for me. Sliding in, I turned to face her.

"That was nice."

"What?"

"The seat." I patted it.

"That's what peace agreements are all about, big sis."

"I think I like peace agreements, then."

Lanie snorted. "I'll bet. Just wait till you have to start doing nice stuff for me. Then you might not feel so eager to have a peace agreement anymore."

"I always do nice stuff for you," I argued as the car pulled out of the drive, passing Natasha on her bike, her breath puffing into frosty clouds in the morning air.

"Like what?" Lanie demanded.

"Like I don't hum in your room anymore. I don't take your stuff anymore. I don't borrow your clothes and I especially don't borrow them and then pick up Gray Cat and get hair all over them 'cause you get real mad."

"Not doing mean stuff to me is not the same thing as doing nice stuff for me," Lanie pointed out.

"Girls," Karen said in warning, "this is starting to sound less and less like a peace agreement."

"Girls, don't start," I said in a perfect Simon voice. Lanie giggled and I think Karen might have, too, except she tried to hide it.

At school, Lanie didn't say anything mean as I climbed out of the car, and I ventured a tiny wave. She didn't return it, but at least not saying anything mean was a start. Natasha met me at the corner and hooked her arm through mine like yesterday never happened.

"Natasha, why is Lanie being so nice to me?" I asked as she walked me to my door.

"Because you scared the living daylights out of her and she thought she made you run away."

I stopped walking for just a moment, bobbing my head and humming while I thought about what to say.

Finally, I said, "How come everybody thinks they made me run away? *I* made me run away. They weren't even there when I did it, so how could they have made me?"

"Sometimes being there doesn't have anything to do with it," Tash said. "Sometimes even if you're there, you can't stop things that—" She broke off and looked around like she wanted to hug me, then realized we were at school in full view of everybody. She hugged me, anyway, and I squirmed.

"Have a good day, bug," she said, although she rarely called me by that nickname at school. With a pat and a wave, she sent me into my classroom and wove her way into the crowded hall behind me.

In my class, G met me at the door with words already chosen and arranged on her Velcro strip: a photo of me wearing the green-and-yellow shirt I wore on the second day of school last year, followed by a cartoon drawing of a stick-figure person running away from a stick-figure house. G's face was accusing as she handed me the strip.

"I did *not* run away," I protested. "I just went to check something out and I got . . . stuck. How did you know? Natasha?"

G nodded impatiently. The ripping-Velcro noise used to hurt my ears, but I had gotten used to it by now. G was rough and wild with her Velcro strip, always in a hurry to talk. She pressed the strip into my hand again: a picture of a stick figure with a horrified expression on its face, followed by a picture of a stick figure sitting on a bench.

"Yes. Stuck because I was scared."

She looked at me gloatingly. Sometimes I thought it made G extraordinarily happy when she guessed right about my feelings. I guess because I was so dismally awful at guessing right about them myself.

Her next pictures were softer and so was her expression. A smiling face, then two hands with palms upturned, the sign for "now."

I smiled back. "Yeah. I'm better now."

G grinned and began putting together another sentence. I knew this one would be about something totally different, because she understood me better than anyone. I wanted to keep talking to G because she was helping me practice for everyone else. Sometimes when I spoke out loud, it was like I had strung random words together into a mockery of a sentence. They made sense in my head, but when I was finished, everyone was staring at me like I had spoken in tongues like the scary ladies at the church we used to go to, and nobody could understand a word I said. G was never like that. She always got it.

She was about to hand me her strip again when I began to sense someone else in my presence, someone else soaking up some of my personal space. I didn't recognize the information my senses were giving me—the smell, the height, the attitude. I didn't recognize the person.

Turning quickly, I stepped back so suddenly I tripped on the trash can and almost fell. As I shouted and grabbed the coat hooks for balance, I sensed motion where the new person had been standing and I flattened myself to the wall, unreasonably afraid. I didn't like it when new people moved quickly.

The new person was nearly as short as G, and round in a way that was comforting. I found her silver hair startling because of how silver it was, and her eyes were just the same.

"I didn't mean to scare you," she said. "I guess I should have properly introduced myself before we met. That way we wouldn't have been strangers."

It took me a minute to puzzle out that she was kidding, and by the time I had, my body had pushed itself up off the wall and my feet had carried me a couple of steps back into what Miss Mandy explained was a polite conversational distance.

"I'm Mrs. Rhodes. I'm the new sub."

I looked behind her as though maybe she were hiding the old sub. "Where's Mrs. Paxton?"

The sound of Velcro ripping, although I was accustomed to it, made me jump when my attention had been so focused on the new person. It was two of the pictures I'd already seen this morning: the scared face and the stick figure running away. G was grinning from ear to ear.

"Mrs. Paxton won't be joining us today," Mrs. Rhodes explained kindly. "I'm going to be here instead. Now, what's your name, dear?"

"Olivia Lashea Owen." I said it all in a rush because that was how I'd learned it.

"Olivia, hmm? Come again?" She leaned closer, making me lean back, which she noticed right away and adjusted herself back to her previous position. "I'm sixty-five, dear. You need to slow down."

"Olivia Lashea Owen," I said slower.

"Well, Olivia Lashea Owen, I heard tell that Michael and Robert just brought the breakfast basket down from the kitchen. Are you hungry?"

"She eats at home," Michael said helpfully from the kitchen. "Always at home."

"I think I'll take some breakfast this morning," I said quickly. "I didn't actually have any at home this morning. I had to run outside and hide in the car."

Mrs. Rhodes tilted her head as if she were slightly confused by this, but she let it pass. As we walked to the kitchen, she asked, "Now, surely you don't go by Olivia Lashea Owen all day long. Is there a shorter name I can call you? Lashea perhaps? Or Ms. Owen?"

I giggled, the kind you do when you're nervous. "Livvie."

"Everyone calls her Livvie." Michael helped again. "She doesn't like her O or her A."

"I don't like my O or my A," I repeated. "They make my name too long and, anyway, Tash started calling me Livvie and I like what Tash calls me."

Mrs. Rhodes began stacking limp blueberry waffles onto a small paper tray. "And who's this Tash? Should I be watching for her?"

"Natasha's my sister. She's one of my two sisters, I mean. I have two sisters." Sometimes my mouth kept talking when my brain was already finished. "How many . . . sisters do you have?" I was pretty sure that wasn't the question I had intended on asking.

"Oh, well, let's see. Counting the one in Florida . . . the one in Illinois and the one in Timbuktu . . . I have no sisters." She smiled wide. "I do have a brother, though. Otis Andrews. Otis is a divine creature. Paints murals. Great, giant pictures he has to climb up scaffolding to paint. I'm quite certain he's going to fall right on his head before the year is out, but Otis never lets that stop him."

I slid slowly into the chair Mrs. Rhodes indicated and she settled the waffles on the table in front of me. "Here you are, dear. Fresh from the kitchen. 'Fresh' being relative, of course."

I liked yogurt best, or Natasha's bagels, but I took a tentative bite of the waffle. It was limp and lukewarm. I smiled thinly at Mrs. Rhodes.

"That good, huh?" she asked briskly. "Well, here, let me have that." She whisked it back off the table. "Who wants yogurt?"

Everybody except for Michael wanted yogurt. Michael liked limp blueberry waffles because they were what he always had on Fridays.

The yogurt was vanilla and Mrs. Rhodes stirred granola bits down into it. It would have been difficult to sip, what with the granola floating around, so I used a spoon. It clacked uncomfortably against my teeth, but the yogurt made it worth it. It tasted extra good.

Having unexpected yogurt when I thought I was going to have to eat a soggy blueberry waffle made the day better by several degrees. There was almost no pressure built up inside my head and I felt relaxed and happy. I was even feeling kind enough to say good morning to Bristol when she entered, although normally we gave each other nothing but suspicious glances. She was wearing warm colors today, so I figured it was safe.

With a startled look, Bristol said an uncertain "Hi . . ." before she and Robert went off to the corner to eat their yogurt and granola without associating with the rest of us.

Mrs. Rhodes helped Peyton eat some yogurt without the granola, and Peyton made a squealing sound and rocked her chair back and forth.

"Is it good, love?" I heard Mrs. Rhodes ask her softly. Shyly, so no one would notice, I watched Peyton's face. Her warm brown eyes kept finding Mrs. Rhodes and then slipping away nervous, like she wasn't sure how to say thank you for the yogurt. I knew how she felt, because I wasn't quite sure how to say thank you for the yogurt, either. I sat and thought about it so long, Mrs. Rhodes finished with Peyton and sat down next to me.

"So, what does this class do after breakfast?" she asked me. "Do we have some sort of a schedule we follow?"

"I have a picture schedule you can look at," I offered, "but you have to promise to give it back."

She smiled a slight, crooked sort of smile. "I would be happy to give it back, of course, but it would be most helpful if you would share."

Jumping up so hard I banged the table and drew a vicious glare from Michael, I galloped to my study carrel and lifted my picture schedule out from under Monday's newsprint scraps.

"Hey! It's not set up!" The pressure was back all of a sudden.

"Of course it's not, dummy!" Bristol yelled. "Mrs. What's-her-head didn't know to do it and the old sub ran away!"

I slammed my picture schedule down on the desk, hard. "What am I supposed to do with no schedule?" I hollered, my voice feeling thin and cracking.

G followed me to the study carrel and tapped me once, but I didn't like touch when I was already full of pressure, and I jumped away from her. "Hey! Watch it!"

Stepping back with narrowed eyes, G put her hands on her hips.

Mrs. Rhodes came a little closer, but not so much that she overwhelmed me again. "May I borrow that schedule?" she asked calmly.

"It's not going to help you! It's blank!"

"What's blank about it? I see pretty white Velcro dots and a lot of potential. Let me see." Her voice stayed calm. I could sense Mr. Raldy lurking nearby, ready to intervene if asked, and I scooted away from him, frustrated by his presence. G ventured closer again and offered me her Velcro strip. I didn't take it because I didn't want to listen right now, but I did see the words she had chosen. A picture of G, smiling, from earlier this year—she liked new pictures a lot—and a picture of a right fist being lifted by a left hand—the sign for "help."

"How?" I demanded.

"Oh, Georgia has offered to help? Fantastic." Mrs. Rhodes smiled at G gratefully. "You'll know the schedule well enough to help me, won't you?"

G nodded and handed Mrs. Rhodes her own picture schedule, which G was organized enough to be in charge of. Hers was always in the proper order, neatly arranged. She did it first thing when she got to school in the mornings. Sometimes I wished I could be like G.

Working my fingers into my hair, I nonetheless did not pull. G looked at me disapprovingly and my insides felt like I had swallowed snakes. She and Mrs. Rhodes sat down calmly at my desk and began preparing my schedule to look like G's.

After several deep breaths, I realized that the pressure had started to diminish again.

"Livvie, tell them you're sorry," I said quietly after a minute. "I'm sorry. I didn't mean to get mad. I got scared."

"Fear makes a person act angry sometimes when

they really feel scared," Mrs. Rhodes said matter-of-factly without looking up. "Now, Livvie, you've got half-eaten yogurt in the kitchen and you've got this fabulous friend here who's willing to help you fix your schedule, so really, I think that all is not lost."

I rocked and hummed for a moment, then replied, "I think you're right." And although neither of us particularly liked them, I gave G a quick hug in thanks.

Velcro ripped and she pressed the strip into my hand.

I knew the pictures well. They meant *You're silly.*

Mrs. Rhodes finished with my schedule and gave G's back to her. Standing, she cupped my cheek in her hand for a moment. Her hands were hot and papery and I didn't like the touch, but it would have been rude to draw away and I had been rude enough for one morning before the bell.

"You really quite remind me of Otis Andrews," she said with a soft sort of smile.

"Does Otis Andrews get mad like Livvie?" I asked.

"Sometimes, dear. But remember what we figured out? I think mostly he just gets afraid."

I nodded wearily and at last couldn't keep myself from drawing away from her touch.

"I'll finish my yogurt and wash the bowl," I said. "That's what you do when you finish, you wash the bowl." I blushed a little. She was in her sixties and probably knew what to do when you finish with a bowl.

"That sounds like a lovely idea, my dear," Mrs. Rhodes said, and with a smile for G and a softer one for me, she headed back to the kitchen.

Chapter 8

I worked on my real estate notebook for almost fifteen minutes before lunch. I accepted Mr. Raldy's real estate pages even though there was a Neighbor-with-an-E section in it. This portion, I separated carefully with my scissors and folded into seven tiny squares before I threw it in the trash can.

Nabor-with-an-A's rental section usually got ignored, since it was the sale houses I was interested in, but it occurred to me this was the section the Sun House was most likely to appear in. The problem was that the words were too hard, and this part didn't have any pictures. Instead each ad began with a bold-print number and some letters, followed by a lot of letters that didn't look like actual words.

Difficult enough even for a reader. I knew be-

nant
rs
3 N.
Wal-
ing

3 BR 1.5 BA North Main
$550/mo. + utils. 555-4811
before 8 PM

EO
V
Cal
GRAP
Med
COM
ect
ct

cause I made Bristol try once and she never got past the bold print.

It never occurred to me to ask a teacher before, but Mrs. Rhodes was different from most teachers, so I followed her through the classroom as she readied us for lunch.

"What's three BR mean?"

"Come again?" She distributed three lunch boxes to three students without looking. It seemed to be a talent that came natural to teachers.

"The paper says there's a house for rent that's three BR, one point five BA."

"Three bedroom, one and a half bath, dear." She helped Robert on with his coat and coaxed Michael to leave all but one of his snake pictures behind, so he had a hand free to eat.

I didn't like the sound of "half bath." It made me

think of our leaky bathtub in the trailer. Counting in my head, I figured out that any ad about the Sun House would have to start with 4 BR and 1 BA. No halves. I scanned the rental section without luck.

We visited the cafeteria between lunch shifts, so it wasn't busy and full of people. I liked it quiet in the cafeteria because when it was even the littlest bit loud, the walls amplified the sound and it got extra loud and echoey. It hurt my ears some and it made me a little upset, but it really killed Michael. He just could not tolerate it. Peyton, too, seemed to dislike the louder noise, and she got louder when it was loud. Her singsongy sounds became shrieks and she banged her head on the back of her chair.

Our peer helper came with us to lunch. His name was Jamie and he was a junior like Natasha. I liked him better than the peer helper who came during second period. Her name was Kristin and she was giggly and flirty and liked to hang around the most with Bristol and Robert, if she could be bothered to hang around with anyone at all. Mostly she just snuck her hands under the table and sent text messages back and forth with her boyfriend.

Jamie helped us get our trays, except he didn't have to help me or G because we were very careful to get it right. He did have to help Michael or Michael would take all of one food and none of the

next, and then get to his table and get frustrated because he only had one kind of food. Michael was
not a planning-ahead sort of guy when it came to
practical matters.

Jamie sat next to G and helped her open her
milk, which was hard for her. "Hey, G, what's up,
girl?" he asked happily, nudging her with his elbow.
He and G were buddies. I wished I knew how to be
buddies.

Velcro ripped, even though G had been told time
and again that talking and eating were not compati-
ble, particularly if you used picture exchange. But
then again, Jamie had asked.

G must have said there wasn't much up, because
Jamie shook his head. "Not much? But aren't you
going to the pep rally Friday?"

G bounced in her seat and giggled. She was girly
when it came to things like pep rallies. She liked
to watch the cheerleaders and she especially liked to
watch the football players.

I rolled my eyes and smiled at them, then let my
gaze slide away. I was just about to take a bite of
my grilled cheese sandwich when I heard the paper
mill whistle, as loud and clear as if the lunch lady
had done it. I dropped my sandwich and bumped the
table. My spoon clattered to the floor so loud that
Peyton shrieked and Michael clapped his hands over

his ears, knocking over his milk with his elbow. Bristol screamed and leapt clear of the spilled milk as it threatened to soak into her warm colors, and her scream inspired an even louder shriek from Peyton. In two instants, the paper mill whistle had demolished the relative quiet of the lunchroom, and all hell had broken loose, courtesy of me.

The noise was so loud, I stood up and backed away. It would help if the whistle would stop blowing, but it blasted away just as merry as ever, although no one else at the table seemed to hear it.

"I have to ask Tash if she heard it!" I yelled, and jumped up from the table as the whistle finally faded. I ran through the cafeteria, ducking around tables and jumping over chairs, bolting down the hallway before anyone could stop me. I knew Natasha's schedule because she showed it to me on the first day of school in case I ever needed to find her. She was worried about high school being a place I could get into trouble and, thinking back on the pandemonium in the cafeteria, I guessed she was right.

This was third period for her because she had already eaten lunch. Blasting through the door, I knocked into a desk right inside the classroom door.

Natasha jumped up from her seat, her face turning red as she glanced around at her openmouthed friends. "Livvie, what are you doing?" she demanded in horror.

"Did you hear it?" I demanded, grabbing her arm. "Did you?"

"Hear what?"

"The whistle!"

"Livvie, for godsake, not this again!" With a firm arm on my shoulder, she guided me back into the hallway. Over her shoulder, she said to her teacher, "Excuse me just for a minute. My sister—"

"Go ahead," the teacher said kindly, as though Natasha were someone to be pitied. I was beside myself about the whistle, but I had time to cast the teacher a hateful glance at his attitude.

In the hallway, Natasha ran her hands down my shoulders and looked me in the eye. "You may not," she said in a shaky voice, "run away from your class to tell me things. And you may not barge into *my* class right in the middle unless it's a life-or-death emergency."

"It *is* an emergency," I insisted. "And you never said it had to be the life-or-death kind!"

"Olivia—" Her eyes rolled away from mine, up to the ceiling, and she took a couple of steadying breaths. "Do you know how awful that looks to have your kid sister come running into your classroom screaming?"

"I wasn't screaming. I was asking and you still haven't answered. Did you?"

"Did I *what*?"

"Hear the whistle!"

"Livvie, there *is* no whistle. The whistle stopped blowing ten years ago. I don't know what you're hearing, but that's not what it is."

"But I *heard* it."

"You heard something." She sighed sharp enough to make her hair blow back. "We all wanted the whistle back, Liv. We all wanted Mom and Dad to keep their mill jobs so they could afford to repair the damage at the Sun House. But it doesn't matter how much you want to hear it. It's gone! You're stressed out about a new teacher and you heard something, but you didn't—you didn't hear what you think you did."

"That's not what I'm stressed out about. I like my new teacher! And you heard it, too, the first time!"

"I was sleeping, Livvie. I was dreaming. That's all. I had a dream." She ran a hand through her hair, much like I did when I was nervous. "Maybe you're just not one of those people who needs to be asleep to have a dream."

I yanked my arm away from her, suddenly suspicious, and began to rock and hum.

"Livvie, you're making things up. You're crazy," I

ventured, knowing this was what Natasha meant to say.

"You're not, you're not crazy, you're just . . . you." She tugged my hands out of my hair. "Stop doing that. Go to class, Livvie. Come on, I'll walk you. I want to make sure you don't run off along the way." Her voice was tired and sounded a lot like Simon's. She took my hand as though I were small.

"Livvie, you didn't hear anything," I said as she walked me toward the cafeteria. I began to hum again, fervently, loud enough I couldn't hear her sighing, except I could sense it, anyway. "You didn't hear anything, so stop hearing things."

Halfway to the lunchroom, we met Mrs. Rhodes and G jogging along the hallway.

"Oh, thank god," Mrs. Rhodes said with a dramatic hand to her forehead. "I really didn't want to lose one on my very first day. Olivia Owen! What were you thinking?"

Velcro ripped, but G's question was along the same lines, only less nice.

"I needed to talk to my sister, only it didn't help."

"Olivia, *want* and *need* are two very different things," Mrs. Rhodes said sternly. "There is never anything that you *need* to do that is more important than being safe, and is running off safe?"

When I didn't answer right away, Natasha
nudged me.

"No," I muttered. Then, "Be polite, Livvie. You're
already in trouble." And a little louder, "No, ma'am."

"That's better," Mrs. Rhodes said briskly. "Well,
now. That's twice today you've bolted away from a
perfectly good plate of food. I'm starting to think
that I make you lose your appetite."

"She usually doesn't have one," Natasha offered.
"I wouldn't blame yourself."

"And you must be the famous Natasha," Mrs.
Rhodes said, changing gears with no obvious warning signs. "You are a popular topic of conversation
with Miss Olivia."

"Maybe a little too popular," Natasha muttered.
"I'm sorry. I told her once that if she ever needed
me . . . and now she thinks she can come find me if
the slightest little thing goes wrong. Like I know
how to fix it." Natasha bit her lip in frustration, ruf-
fling my hair so I knew she didn't hate me.

I hummed harder for a minute as tears filled my
eyes. "Livvie, say you're sorry," I whispered, but I
wasn't quite sure how.

Natasha must have heard me, anyway, because
she gave me a hug, loose and long. Then waved and
walked back toward her class, drawing a shaky

breath as she went and running her hands through her hair.

"She's mad," I said softly as she walked out of sight.

"I think," Mrs. Rhodes said softly, "that you might have frightened your sister. And remember what we said about fear."

I didn't remember, but I nodded, anyway.

We headed back for the cafeteria, where Jamie was helping my classmates clean up their trays and wipe down the tables. Michael was standing several feet away, frowning.

"You put milk on my snake," he accused as I approached.

"Nuh-uh, Livvie wasn't even here, I wasn't even here."

"You made it spill." He glared at the shrinking puddle and the rag in Jamie's hand.

I felt worry. "Is your snake ruined?"

"It lived, no thanks to you. Snake pictures are paper and when paper gets wet, it bends and it gets easier to tear, so you could have killed my snake easy, and then I would have only had one hundred forty-seven pictures of snakes instead of one hundred forty-eight, and I wouldn't have a single ratsnake. You suck!"

The term "ratsnake" made me shiver, and Michael's anger made my eyes feel wet. Jamie patted my shoulder as he passed to usher Michael and the others out of the lunchroom.

The bell rang as I sat down and I automatically stood up again.

"No, sit, sit," Mrs. Rhodes insisted, and she sat next to me, G on her other side. "The three of us are going to be late to gym today. We have some eating to do! Mr. Raldy and Jamie are perfectly capable of taking the class to P.E."

It made me nervous to stay in the lunchroom after the bell, especially when it started to fill up with loud people. I ate fast and threw the rest away.

Velcro ripped as I finished. The cartoon face was smiling, the hand in the universal symbol for "OK."

"You're not mad?" I asked G.

Her next words were along the lines of "Never at Livvie."

I smiled. That wasn't true, but she was sweet for saying it. I hugged her tight for the second time that day, and we headed off to gym hand in hand. Mrs. Rhodes walked behind us, humming to herself. She was the only person I'd met other than me who hummed in public.

Natasha didn't wait for me outside after school that day. It was Simon who picked us up today, still wearing his blue Walmart shirt with the smiley face on the pocket.

"Hey there," he said as I climbed into the car. "How was school?"

"I'm not crazy, right?" I said by way of answer, and Simon closed his eyes for half a second and rubbed his stubble.

"That good, huh?" he asked with a sigh.

Lanie had taken the front seat this time, but she cast me a half-apologetic smile. I piled in behind her, dragging my full book bag behind me. I had spent an extra lot of time today pasting real estate ads into my notebook after gym.

"Where's Natasha?" Simon asked, surveying the crowd for her.

"She's over there," Lanie said before I could, and I spun quickly and saw that she was right. Natasha had been watching me from the corner the entire time.

My stomach suddenly felt very sick and upset. Natasha had waited to make sure I was safe, I thought, but she hadn't wanted to talk to me.

"I made her mad today," I said, and began to hum.

"Oh my god, please don't start humming," Lanie said from the front seat. "Remember we're in a peace agreement and this is one of those nice things you have to do for me."

"I feel like I'm going to blow," I said faintly. "I have to do something and humming is mild. That's what Miss Mandy always said." I worked my hands into my hair again.

"Yeah, it was so mild it chased her out of town," Lanie muttered, and I hummed louder.

"Seriously, don't start that," Simon said. "I mean it, Livvie." He drove a little faster. "Let's just get ourselves home with no fighting and no humming and no hair-pulling, okay?"

I pressed my hands against my head instead and began tightening my joints as hard as I could, one after another. After a minute I noticed Lanie watching me in the mirror.

"What are you saying?" she asked when we made eye contact.

I hadn't realized I was talking, or rather, mouthing silent words into the car.

"Sometimes scared looks the same as mad," I said faintly. "That's what Mrs. Rhodes said. I just remembered." My eyes strayed to Simon.

"Who's Mrs. Rhodes?"

"My new sub."

"Gawd, you guys scared off another one?" Lanie bounced on her seat. "That's, like, a record. I think I'm impressed."

"Lanie," Simon said in warning tones, but I actually thought it was funny what Lanie was saying. Then to me, "What's the new one like?"

"Tougher than the others," I said promptly. "She might stick awhile." Simon laughed in surprise as though he hadn't expected this type of assessment from me. "She gave me yogurt," I added, "and she didn't get mad when I—" I pulled up short. I had been about to say something about running to Natasha's classroom, but suddenly it didn't seem like a good idea to pass that on to Simon just when he was getting over being mad at me. "—when I got nervous," I amended.

"Well, that's a good sign," he said. "Did she help you do your picture schedule?"

"G helped, too. I got scared, but G helped."

"G's sister goes to my school," Lanie said unexpectedly.

"Really?"

"She's a seventh grader, though. She doesn't like me very much. She thinks I'm annoying."

A part of me wanted to say, "You are annoying," but I was pretty sure that didn't fit into a peace agreement. So instead I said, "She must not be very much like G."

The Tercel bumped uncomfortably into the drive. "I've got to go straight back out," Simon said. "I'm stopping to see a house and then I need to pick up your mother. Lanie, will you help Livvie get her snack?"

"I don't need help," I said a little irritably. "I can get my own snack."

"I want to see the house," Lanie said promptly. "Where is it?"

"Anderson Street." His answer made me whoosh with relief, glad that he hadn't said Neighbor-with-an-E. "And if it's a good one, I'll show you later. Right now I need you to help your sister with her snack."

"I can get my own snack," I repeated.

"I don't want to find out you ate half a cracker and called that a snack," Simon said by way of explanation. "We'll have to eat pretty late tonight. Your mom and I have a meeting at work before we can come home."

I sighed. I hated late dinner. Natasha didn't like sitting at the table with us all if she could help it, and a lot of times Lanie was too busy talking on the phone to her classmates to be bothered sitting with the rest of us, but at least we could have a dinner*time* like an ordinary family, couldn't we? Only Karen's and Simon's work often interfered with that.

"I'll make sure she eats," Lanie said with what I thought might have been an evil twinkle in her eye. I got a little nervous, but I kept my hum to a whisper.

Something stopped me going up the steps. The front door looked different somehow. I couldn't focus on why till Lanie pulled a piece of paper off some tape above the doorknob and stared at it for a moment.

"What is that, what is that?" I asked, nervous enough it came out twice.

"It's from Janna," Lanie said with a mad face. "She wants us to leave her ugly chair when we go." She crumpled it against her thigh with one hand while she unlocked the door with the other.

The inside of the trailer was cold and quiet and I knew that meant Natasha wasn't home yet. Lanie bumped up the heat till it kicked on, then gave me an expression I recognized.

"Don't bump it up any more," she said warningly.

"Aren't we in a peace agreement?" I asked hopefully.

"Even people in peace agreements have to pay electric bills," she said firmly. "No turning it up. Do you want crackers or Doritos for a snack?"

My eyes widened. "You're going to let me have Doritos for a snack?"

"Only if I get to share. This *is* a peace agreement, after all!"

We settled ourselves on the blankets we kept on

the living room floor, ignoring Janna's ugly chair she was afraid we were going to steal. The TV set was old, but it went perfectly with the old VCR Natasha had found us at a yard sale. We had a few favorite videos each, plucked here and there on sale, mostly from the Walmart bargain bin.

As we settled in front of the TV, Lanie tugging a blanket for both of us off the back of the sofa, she looked at me funny. "Did you see what Dad was reading before you got in?"

"A newspaper?"

"It wasn't ours," she said, and I looked up, startled.

"What do you mean?" Thinking she was trying to say he'd stolen it or something.

"It was a Neighbor paper. With an E."

Which might be worse. I thought about this for a moment. "We wouldn't move there."

"Maybe." She sat for a moment. "I think it might be cool if we did. Mom and Dad wouldn't have to drive so far."

"Olivia lives in Nabor," I said firmly. "With an A." My hands automatically went to the worn case of my favorite movie, *Danny*.

"Oh, god, not that again," Lanie said with a groan, and it was clear that her patience with this peace agreement was wearing thin. When I looked at her, she was obliterating all traces of Janna's note with her purple pen. Her face was stressed.

I felt a worried sort of feeling. "But this is my favorite. It's what I always watch after school."

"That's the problem," Lanie said with a loud sigh. "I'm *bored* of this one, Olivia. Don't you get bored with anything?"

"I like things the same. I don't like them different. I don't like them different."

Lanie looked sideways at me and took another Dorito. "There's such a thing as too much 'the same,' you know?"

I wasn't sure I did, but she looked ready to cry, so instead of answering, I put *Danny* back on the shelf. Three deep, steadying breaths and I was able to speak.

"You pick."

She glanced sideways at me again. Then picked *Danny* and left the room.

Chapter 9

I wandered through the broken rooms as though I was looking for something. I knew when I found it. It was Orange Cat again, weaving back and forth among the bits of old furniture and the beams of lumber I hadn't noticed my first time through.

"I'm dreaming again, aren't I?" I asked Orange Cat, and he flattened his ears but didn't hiss at me this time.

"Sorry," I whispered. "Did I break another rule?"

He wouldn't make eye contact with me and I felt rare tears pooling up in my own eyes. "Livvie wishes you would look at her," I whispered.

He swished his tail hard, then trotted, tail up, into the back bedroom, the one that had been mine. I followed with the tears beginning to slip down my face. I remembered this walk. Never mind I was only three when we left this house, I remembered the walk from the kitchen to the bedroom and the way it felt to be a part of this place.

I think I was too little, back at the Sun House, for my parents to know there was anything different about me. But now I was fourteen, I was too big to fit through the archways right. I could no longer sit on a closet shelf, all folded up like a rag doll, like I did when I was three. I was practically a grown-up, trespassing here.

Slowly, as I followed Orange Cat, I became aware of voices. They were whispering at first, but they grew in strength and seriousness as I wandered through the rooms. In each room I found more furniture to step over, more giant beams and boards of lumber scattered from the walls to trip my step. Orange Cat leapt lightly over them, but me, I was in trouble. I could hear the whistle even over the voices. I smelled water and something hot. Something was very wrong in this place.

He led me into the bedroom again and this time the plywood was gone from the windows, but the shutters banged and blew in the wind. Shutters? The Sun House didn't have shutters, especially not with moons cut in them like these.

I reached for Orange Cat and he disappeared with one last, mournful look back at me. The tears came at last and I plunked myself onto one of the beams. I cried so hard for Orange Cat that I woke myself up in the dark, hugging Gray Cat so tightly that she hissed.

I was out of bed and halfway down the hallway when I remembered about Natasha being mad at me today. I stopped uncertainly, then thought about altering my course to aim at my parents' room instead, but they were so tired when they got home last night and so stressed out, anyway, that I pictured waking them up and thought I saw them angry in the picture.

My feet chose a destination and I found myself in front of the drinking glass cupboard.

"Rules are rules, Olivia," I whispered. Only this time I was so used to the whistle that if I heard it blow, I knew I would be able to keep from dropping anything.

I was right, too. When the whistle blew, I stayed standing perfectly still on my chair, drawing deeper and deeper breaths and trying to control myself.

But as soon as the whistle stopped blowing, I broke another rule. I put my feet in my socks and my socks in my shoes, because I knew better than slippers and I didn't have any, anyways. No slippers. No mug. No Orange Cat. And Tasha wondered why I'd been so stressed lately! I pulled on my hoodie and made it halfway out the door before somebody grabbed me and I shrieked.

"Shush!" Lanie slapped her hand over my mouth. I yanked out of her grip and shrugged away into my own personal space.

"Livvie heard it again," I said. "I'm not making it up!" I began to hum frantically before she could respond, wrapping my fingers in my hair. I knew her response was going to be an unpleasant one. Lanie shoved us out the door and closed it behind us, so suddenly I had to steady myself on her shoulder to keep from falling backward off the steps.

"Don't wake Mom and Dad," she whispered fiercely. "We'll get in so much trouble if you wake them!"

"Then go with Livvie," I demanded.

She shook her head furiously. "No!"

"Lanie, come with me! You can help me find the whistle!"

"I don't *want* to find the whistle," she said. "It's scary."

It took almost a second for what she said to sink in, but when it did, I stared at Lanie so hard I even forgot to hold on to my hair again. Sinking onto the top step, I pulled a reluctant Lanie down with me.

"You heard it," I accused.

Now it was Lanie's turn to run her hands through

her hair, sighing loudly as she did. Looking up slowly, she made eye contact with me, and her facial expression was something so startling I was glad I didn't have a name for it.

"I dreamt it," she corrected me.

We sat like that for a full minute and then Lanie stood up and grabbed my hand. "Well, come on, then."

"Where are we going?"

"To find it, dummy!"

"But I thought—"

"Come *on* before I come to my senses!" She yanked my hand and I had to jump down three steps to keep from falling flat on my face.

Despite her confidence, once we got past the trailer park gates it was me who took the lead. Lanie's motions became hesitant, like she was frightened being out in the dark like this.

"Livvie, you know the way, right?" I asked, because I knew she wanted to. "Of course I do, or I wouldn't be out here!"

"Livvie, you're silly," Lanie said, but she seemed comforted just the same. Still, she stuck close to me in the darkness. We walked quickly until Lanie slowed as we passed the house on Probart Street, the one with the useless black shutters.

"Did we . . ." She pulled up short. "We did, right?"

"We did. Come and see." I tugged her toward the house.

"Wait, what are you doing? Hey!" She dug in her heels, but I pulled harder. There was a car in the drive and bikes in the yard, so I knew somebody was home, but it was just after midnight and the house was too quiet for anyone to be awake.

This one was easier to find than some, because, instead of writing it in my bedroom, I had written it in my favorite place in the house—the spacious back porch. I started thinking it had been painted over, but it turned out I was just looking too high. A girl could grow a lot in just a few years. At last I found it: *Livvie Owen Live Here,* inscribed forever in black ink, scratched deep.

"God, you even used to write on the walls back then?" Lanie whispered. She stuck her hands in her pockets. Her eyes darted left and right and she was already backing up.

"I write this everywhere," I said impatiently. "I like the houses to remember me."

"You spelled it wrong, you know."

"How did I spell it wrong?"

"You left the 'd' off 'lived.' Anyway, houses don't

remember." She grabbed up a pebble and scratched a d shape after my "live." I added the d shape to my mental picture of what my favorite sentence looked like. Somehow I'd missed that shape when I first learned how to write my sentence.

On Pendleton Street, we started to jog, partly because we were cold and partly because it was darker out here, and creepier than the rest of the walk. At the end of the street, my feet slowed all on their own, and I tugged my little sister to a stop outside the Sun House.

"This is it," I said in a voice like Mr. Raldy making an announcement, not quite loud enough, and a little bit wavering.

"The factory's *there*," she said, pointing, like I was a very small child. "What are you talking about, 'this is it'?"

"This is the Sun House."

Lanie wrinkled her nose. "I know that, dummy. We must have driven past here thirty or forty million times and you always point it out."

"Just from the end of the street, not from up close. You need to see it."

She shook her head. "It's not even yellow."

"But it was. We're going to live here."

Lanie tugged me hard past the Sun House, through the factory's front gates. "Come on. We're going to find this whistle and get home before we get caught."

"But I want to go in the Sun House. We're going to live there!"

"Shut up. Let's just check for the whistle and we'll go home." Her teeth started to chatter. "I don't want to live there. It's creepy and they've never fixed it back." She pulled her hand loose from my grip and ran on ahead, feet scattering gravel across the weedy front lot of the factory.

"Lanie, wait!"

"No! I want to get this over with so we can get out of this creepy place!" Her voice echoed funny and I looked over my shoulder like there might be more than one of her talking. She tried the door of the first building, but it was locked and we both whooshed out a sigh of relief. The windows were broken and only darkness stared back at us through them. I wasn't sure I wanted the door to open.

"You'll want to live there once you see it," I insisted, picking up the conversation as though there hadn't been a pause. "It's so warm inside, Lanie. It's got so many rooms, we could each have our own. And Orange Cat's there. Please come and see!"

Lanie looked at me in surprise, then jogged toward the next building. Her feet made echoey noises against the tin siding of the buildings, and

I hummed to cover it up. Lanie looked ready to say something but then she tried another door and we both leapt back when this one swung open with a shriek of metal.

We slid to a halt and my hum died in my throat. Despite walking here in the dark, despite Lanie's efforts at the doors, neither one of us had anticipated actually getting a door to open.

Inside the building loomed darkness. Lanie shivered and hugged herself. I hung back behind her. Despite our bickering, we scooted closer to each other in the dark. Her hand found mine and I squeezed it.

"Do you—do you think it came from in here?" she asked hesitantly, her voice a little smaller than before.

"I don't know which building it came from," I admitted. "I think maybe the Sun House."

Lanie didn't even look at me. "You're not making any sense," she said flatly. "The Sun House doesn't have a whistle." She was shivering in her pajamas and her purple sweatshirt. I realized too late that I should have at least made her put on a coat.

"Should we go in?" I asked, just as the wind made the door shriek again.

"I think maybe we should go back in time and rethink this plan instead." Lanie stomped one foot and backed up a step. "Forget this!" She spun in the gravel and began trotting toward home. Now that I was alone, the gaping doorway seemed darker than ever. The night was suspiciously silent. I thought bizarrely that if this was where I was supposed to go, the whistle would have blown again.

Several feet ahead, Lanie stopped, dancing from foot to foot, looking back over her shoulder. Beyond her I could make out the shapes of the fence line and the overgrown trees that had only been saplings when we lived here. The Sun House loomed darker than the darkness of the sky, and it, too, was silent, no whistle to speak of.

"Liv," Lanie said in a tiny voice. "Please. Please, let's get out of here. It's creepy."

She was right. It *was* creepy, worse than cough syrup, worse than wet slippers. I followed her back across the crumbled sidewalk to the factory gate and she tugged me with her past the Sun House without slowing down.

"But we have to stop!"

"No! You're being stupid! We aren't going to stop!" Something about her voice made me fearful and sorry, way inside. My eyes cast toward the Sun House, toward the sign that had blown down off the rail and now lay facedown on the porch.

I tugged at Lanie, hard. "Just read the sign."

Suddenly taken with the desire to know for certain what it said.

"I'm going home!"

"Please, just read the sign—"

"Let's go," she pleaded, her eyes flooding with tears. It had been years since I had made my sister cry in anything other than frustration. I had a hunch our peace agreement had not survived our midnight journey. "This was really stupid. Please, let's go."

"Okay," I whispered finally, eyes drifting hopelessly toward the sign on the porch. It stayed upside down, out of reach. Beyond it lay a house that, according to my dreams, contained my Orange Cat. But he was mad at me, anyway. I patted her awkwardly. "Okay, Lane."

"Okay," she repeated in a shaky voice. "I'm never listening to you again." Yet she clung fast to my hand as we ran back the way we'd come, cutting a frightened path through a quiet night.

Chapter 10

My brother, Otis Andrews, always says the same thing."

This was Mrs. Rhodes, insisting that I sit down for a hot breakfast even though I ate at home.

"But I'm really *not* hungry!" I explained. I was busy scanning Mr. Raldy's rental section for any 4 BR, 1 BA ads.

"Excuse me! Was I finished talking?"

"No, ma'am," I squeaked, having discovered already that it was far better to let Mrs. Rhodes finish her stories than to interrupt her.

"Thank you. Ahem. Like I was saying. My brother, Otis Andrews, always says he isn't hungry, and then I make him sit down and he eats four or five pieces of toast and an egg before he even starts to slow down. Now, does that sound like 'not hungry' to you, young lady? Does it?"

"No, ma'am," I repeated, sighing as I reluctantly took the bagel she insisted on handing me.

"Is your brother . . . you know . . ." Jamie asked. His eyes slid to me and away again quickly. I wondered what Mrs. Rhodes knew that I didn't, because I didn't understand quite what he was asking. Bristol, in her warm colors, stopped eating and looked up as if she understood and wanted to know the answer.

"My brother is a lot of things," Mrs. Rhodes said briskly. "He has a boatload of artistic talent. He has autism. And he has the loudest snore of anyone I've ever met."

"That's what I have, autism," I said faintly. "Your brother does, too?"

"Yes. But the more important question is, do you snore as loud as Otis Andrews?"

I giggled in spite of my sleepiness and my bad mood. "No, ma'am, I hope not," I said.

Three bites into the bagel, I managed to slide it into the trash without being caught, or so I thought until Mrs. Rhodes tsk-tsked at me. But she didn't say anything else.

G was sticking close to me this morning as if she sensed my mood. At last she handed me her Velcro strip with a picture of a girl yawning on it.

"Yes, I'm sleepy," I said in an undertone, hoping Mrs. Rhodes wouldn't pick up on it.

No such luck. "And why is that, dear?" she asked.

"No reason," I said sharply.

"Good. I hope you weren't breaking any rules last night. I saw a silhouette that looked much like you on my neighbor's back porch last night, but maybe I was only dreaming."

My eyes widened huge. "You live on Probart Street?"

"My dear, whoever said anything about Probart Street?" she asked, then tsk-tsked again, and I knew I'd been caught.

"Livvie, you've done it now," I said. Then, "Are you going to tell Tash? 'Cause she's still real mad at me for yesterday."

"Are you asking me or Livvie?" Mrs. Rhodes said gently. Then answered, "No, I won't tell Natasha. I imagine she has quite enough to worry about without my adding to the list."

I wasn't sure what she meant by this, so I settled myself at the table. I was very curious about this idea of Otis Andrews having autism.

"Was he always like that?" I asked. It took Mrs. Rhodes a moment to figure out what I was talking about.

"Oh, Otis?" she asked after a moment. "My, yes.

He painted from the very first day he was old enough to hold on to a paintbrush. Before that, he painted in his own drool on the high chair." She shuddered. "I never particularly liked that habit, but you know, you just can't stop an artist."

I wrinkled my nose in disgust, but refused to be distracted from my question.

"I meant have autism. Did he always do that?"

"Did he always have autism? Yes, I believe he did. Of course, they didn't call it that at first. They called it 'slow,' which was quite incorrect, as he could think circles around me even as a baby. But autism seems to be something you either have or you don't, like blue eyes or a crooked chin." She tugged her own crooked chin and smiled sideways at me.

"Me, too," I said. "I've always had autism, too."

"I do not like that word," Michael said with sudden stress in his voice. "We don't use that word in this classroom, okay?" He walked out of the kitchen before anyone could answer. I could hear him in the next room, banging the cabinets while he looked for his science magazines with the pictures of the snakes, glossy and smooth. I knew he would sit and stroke their scales until his pressure went away again.

"Michael, too," I confided. "But he doesn't like it and I don't blame him."

"Well, why on earth do you say that?"

"It makes life pretty crazy," I explained, and downed the last of my juice.

"I've got news for you, sweet Livvie," Mrs. Rhodes said, whisking the crumbs off the table with a napkin. "Life's pretty crazy, even when you don't have autism."

"But you have a brother with autism and that's the same thing. You had to deal with your brother growing up and you had to keep him out of trouble, right?"

"He was the best big brother anyone could ask for," Mrs. Rhodes said briskly. "Both growing up and now."

"He's your big brother?"

"Yes."

"I thought he was younger."

She shook her head. "Older by two years."

"But you take care of him."

She shook her head matter-of-factly as though this had no bearing on anything. "That's what siblings do," she said. "They take care of each other. You take care of your sisters, don't you?" She walked out of the kitchen to help G, who was having trouble wiggling out of her sweatshirt. I was left in the kitchen by myself, watching the sink drip.

"Don't you?" I asked, very quietly, so nobody but myself would hear. "Well, Livvie? Don't you?"

But nobody answered.

A few minutes before lunch, I slipped away. Only for a second, and I knew better, but it wasn't anything bad this time. Natasha wasn't in class, she should be coming back from lunch, and all I did was stand in the hallway until I saw her coming.

"Are you loitering, Livvie?" She saw me before I intended her to and I didn't quite have what I wanted to say planned out.

"I was waiting for you."

"Again?" She sounded tired. "We talked about this."

I hummed, stopped myself. "Do I take care of you?"

She tilted her head, puzzled. "What do you mean, bug?"

"Mrs. Rhodes says siblings take care of each other. She takes care of her older brother, who has autism like me. She says he takes care of her, too, because that's what siblings do. Do I take care of you?"

I counted six separate emotions as they flitted across her features, but I couldn't label any of them. Then her shoulders slumped and a sigh went out of her and she pulled me into her arms.

"Of course you do, honey" was all she said.

I still had this funny feeling in my stomach, like maybe she was making it up. But she turned me around and headed me back through the double doors before I could ask anything further.

"Lost one," she called to Mrs. Rhodes, who was helping Mr. Raldy with Peyton's feeding tube.

Mrs. Rhodes paled when she realized what Natasha meant. "Oh, dear," she said. "Oh, my, Livvie, I'm going to put a bell on you, my girl, that's exactly what I'm going to do. Get over here." She grabbed me in an uncomfortable hug and then looked at me. "Why do you keep doing this to me?"

"It wasn't to you. You were busy. I knew Natasha would be walking by and I had a question."

"Olivia Owen, I have known you for forty-eight hours and you have given me forty-eight brand-new gray hairs." She squinted in a funny sort of way. "There is a rule. It might be a new rule and it might not, but it is a rule from this point on. You are *not* to leave this room without telling an *adult*. No, not telling, *asking*. And getting permission and filing a flight plan for exactly where you will be going and exactly when you will be coming back and then you will not be taking detours. And that, young lady, goes for leaving your *house* as well. Do we understand each other?"

I had begun to rock and hum as she spoke, feeling the nervous energy pouring off her, but Natasha nudged me and I responded.

"Yes, ma'am." Point taken, no matter how nervous it made me.

"Thank you," Natasha said to Mrs. Rhodes.

"Thank *you,* sweetie." Mrs. Rhodes gave Natasha a pat and it seemed to me suddenly odd that the two of them—the mid-sixties substitute teacher and the sixteen-year-old junior in high school—had something in common.

Peyton squealed and Mrs. Rhodes turned her attention back to my classmate as G approached me.

"Stop being stupid," her Velcro strip said, but I understood how she meant it and I didn't get offended.

"I'm trying," I whispered urgently. "I'm really trying, but I just can't seem to get a handle on it!"

For some reason, G thought this was the funniest thing she'd ever heard, and she bounced onto the sofa with her face in her hands, giggling gleefully. Although I didn't get the joke, I smiled uncertainly at her and took a seat next to her, waiting for my teachers to work out the problem with Peyton so they could join me at the worktable.

As the day wore on, though, I found that I could not shake my thoughts of the issues Mrs. Rhodes had brought up about her brother. *Was* I helpful to my siblings? Maybe not, judging from Natasha's guarded reaction. And maybe it was okay, I thought, not to be so helpful to Natasha—after all, she was older than me.

But Lanie was younger, just like Mrs. Rhodes was younger than Otis Andrews. Wasn't I supposed to be a big sister to Lanie and help her out as much as possible?

One thing was certain, I thought as I met Natasha at the corner of the school that afternoon. I was definitely *not* going to ask Lanie. After last night's adventures, I wasn't sure I was tough enough to take whatever answer she would give me.

At home, I found Gray Cat asleep in the center of the small kitchen table. Brushing her off with a scolding, I scooped her up almost immediately and apologized.

"You're not supposed to be on the table, okay?" I said, scratching her cheek the way she liked best. She crooked her head sideways and began to purr, reluctantly at first, but gaining strength when I headed her toward the bedroom and her food bowl.

I had barely unpacked my real estate catalogs when a noise drew my attention from down the hallway. In Natasha and Lanie's room, I found Lanie standing in the center of the room looking around.

155

"Why does she do this?" she asked me. "Why does she pick up my stuff and put it away? *I'm* going to pick up my stuff and put it away, if she just *gives* me a minute or two! She always complains that I never clean up my room, but then she never gives me a chance! She just does it for me like she's my mother or something! What is her *problem*?" She stomped her foot, hard, and it struck me again that a sixteen-year-old and an eleven-year-old should not be sharing a room.

Wordlessly, I turned and wandered back down the hall toward my room. I learned long ago not to interfere with my little sister when she was already upset. But the problem of her living situation—and the reason for it—plagued me again as I tried to settle down with my real estate catalogs.

Of course her living situation paled in comparison to our collective living situation, I realized as I stopped myself from counting down the days. Knowing the actual number of days we had left only made them go by faster, and it was already going to take every single one of them to find the perfect vacant home in Nabor-with-an-A.

I opened my real estate catalog and immediately closed it. My hands felt restless and began the finger play they remembered from that night waiting on the empty bus bench in the rain. I didn't know why, but I was too impatient tonight, too restless and distracted, to work on my catalog. Since Simon and Karen had begun to work extra shifts, the impossibility of affording a house was starting to interfere with my ability to plan one for us.

Instead, I flipped open the rental section, scanning for the right number of bedrooms and bathrooms. There was one, but I recognized the word "Probart" and I knew that wasn't right. In a different ad, I recognized "Pendleton," but the numbers didn't match up. Perhaps the Sun House was being rented through a different catalog, I thought. Perhaps my own catalogs were useless.

I went to bed early and woke several times in the night, each time more wide awake and restless than the last. I reached for Gray Cat in the night, but she got tired of playing my teddy bear and began to fuss each time I woke her, so I finally stopped. For the first time since he'd died, I itched to sneak out and visit Orange Cat's grave, but Mrs. Rhodes had laid down some very specific rules about leaving the house, and I was not about to break them.

I wanted to go to Natasha, but something I didn't have words for stopped me.

So I thought of going to Lanie, but that wouldn't work, either. Forcing myself to stay in bed, I stared at the ceiling and counted dots in the ceiling squares till morning while the trailer made night noises around me: creaks with every breeze, the starting and stopping of the electric vent, and dripping from the sink in the bathroom, where a night-light glowed softly through my open bedroom door.

Morning came slowly and by gentle degrees of daylight, and it never developed fully because the weather had changed overnight. Heavy clouds buried the sky and the temperature continued to drop, even as day arrived. I would need two sweaters today. Maybe even a blanket. I had nine to choose from.

At least it was Saturday and I didn't have to freeze my way through a day at Nabor High School. The building and everything in it was ancient and, Bristol and Robert liked to joke, the heating system had been built before winter was invented. It was usually freezing cold in the building, except on the rare days the heat kicked on properly, and on those days, it was sweltering and stuffy.

Since the trailer didn't like to stay warm, I sat with my feet on the vent and my blanket over my feet, so the heat was trapped. Lanie liked to complain that I was stealing all the heat, but this was my bedroom and I didn't care what Lanie thought right this second. I was too cold to care.

Mom found me on the bedroom floor, catching

the heat with my blanket and still counting the holes in the ceiling. I felt sluggish and sleepy today.

"Good morning, Livvie-bug," Mom said, kneeling beside me. "What are you thinking about?"

"Good morning, Karen. I'm thinking about how many holes are in the ceiling. Why is it so freezing out today?"

Karen laughed. "You haven't been out yet. How do you know it's freezing out?"

" 'Cause it's freezing *in*," I explained. "I was so cold last night, I dreamed about seeing my breath. That's pretty cold."

"That is pretty cold." Karen slid down the wall beside me and looped an arm around my shoulders. "So, what's the deal, kiddo?"

"The temperature dropped."

Karen looked at me like she wasn't sure if I was being sarcastic or not. "That's not what I meant, bug."

"What did you mean?"

"I mean your sisters are moping around the house, and they're mad at each other, which *never* happens because Natasha doesn't get mad, hardly. What's going on?"

I moaned softly and leaned my head on Karen's shoulder. "I don't know. I'm so tired, Karen."

She stroked my hair for a minute.

"Did you sneak out with Lanie the other night?"

I puzzled it out for a moment. Understood. "Did Mrs. Rhodes tell you?"

"She wants you to be safe."

"Lanie heard—" I was nervous about saying it anymore, because this was the part where people stared like I was crazy. But it was still the truth and the truth was still what I was supposed to say. "She heard the whistle, too. We wanted to check."

"Oh." My mother's voice was a little higher than usual with stress and maybe like she had tears hidden in there somewhere. She sighed and squeezed me. I wondered if she was mad, but she said, "Did you find anything?" and that was all.

"No. Lanie made me come home. The sign fell off the porch rail."

"What sign?"

"I don't know."

Karen sighed and I felt her shaking a little against me, not like she was shivering but like she was catching her breath, as if she had run somewhere.

"That's all?" she said at last.

"Yes, ma'am."

"And you won't do it again, Livvie. Right?"

"Yes, ma'am—I mean—no, ma'am."

"Because you said that last time."

"This time I promise."

"Okay." She rested her head on my shoulder for a minute, then stood. I let her go and listened to her walking back into the kitchen.

I sat for longer than I intended, longer than my usual Saturday schedule would allow. For some reason, my schedule felt off today and that felt all right with me. Saturday mornings were reserved for alone time with my real estate catalogs, but this morning, I couldn't bring myself to face the pictures in the catalogs with their neat, even windows and their pretty curtains that probably didn't come with the houses, anyway.

I couldn't bring myself to face our own home, either, when our days in it were numbered. I had to get out. But Orange Cat's grave was lonely in the autumn daylight. We'd marked it with a stone on which I'd painted Orange Cat's name and age, but the paint washed off in the subsequent rain and now Orange Cat was remembered with just a cold gray stone. There was litter nearby from the neighbors. I picked it up a piece at a time and ran it back into the house to put in the trash. At some point, without really thinking about it, that's where I put my real estate catalogs, too. My heavy notebook made a thunk when I dropped it on top.

I stood there for a minute, looking into the trash

can, every bit as reverent as I was at Orange Cat's grave. The notebook didn't mean much now, not with the sign outside the Sun House, but it knew my hands so well that I couldn't help reaching in to touch it one last time.

Simon went out before lunch and came back an hour later looking a good bit happier than he had in days.

"Found a good one," he said. "Clear over on the other side of town, just off Pendleton Street. It couldn't hurt to look."

"A rental?" Lanie sat up straighter, looking much more cheerful than she had moments ago, moping at the table, not looking at Natasha or me. "Can we go look now?"

"As soon as everyone finishes eating."

All eyes turned to my lettuce and mayonnaise sandwich with three bites taken out of it. Swallowing with difficulty, I glanced around at my family and quickly dumped the rest of the sandwich in the trash.

"I'm finished," I volunteered.

It was rare the whole family squeezed together in the Tercel, and when we did, it was a tight fit. Driving across town, I registered, took a lot less time than walking. We got there at one and parked in front of a small gray house with an even smaller porch. The house had a friendly face, but of course it was nowhere near as big as the houses in the Neighbor real estate catalogs I had thrown away this morning. The yard was mostly dirt, but you could tell there would be grass later when the weather was warm and the winter had passed.

Simon lifted the planter on the front porch to reveal the key. "Landlord said we could unlock it, look around. Then contact him if we're interested. He was the first pet-friendly, kid-friendly person I talked to, and the price really isn't that bad for a house this size." He said it like the house was big, but I was mentally counting windows.

"It might not have enough rooms, Olivia," I whispered, "so don't get your hopes up." Humming my way up the front steps, I followed my sisters into the living room.

"Good, sturdy structure," Simon said.

"And clean," Karen added with hope in her voice. My parents got good over the years at making even the most dismal home seem suitable, in case it was all we could find.

But I didn't like the ceilings, hanging too low. Simon had to duck to get from the living room to the kitchen and I didn't think he would remember to do that at midnight in his boxers, so I could imagine several nights of bumped heads and rising tempers.

"I don't like this place," I announced.

"Bug, give it a chance," Natasha said quickly. "Come on, let's go check out the bedrooms." Her eyes on my parents were nervous.

My suspicions were correct: There were only three bedrooms. That meant Natasha and Lanie would still have to share if we moved in.

"But this won't work," I protested as Natasha began outlining which room would belong to whom while Lanie darted from room to room, checking views out of windows, planning contents of built-in bookshelves before we could even be sure they would be ours. "This is three BR, one BA. That's not big enough."

"I like it," Lanie said, ignoring my assessment. "Our bedroom is huge!"

"You don't have a bedroom here yet," I protested. "Tash, I don't like it."

"Okay, try to be specific. What don't you like about it?" Natasha, also ducking to get through the doorways, sounded more open than Lanie to my critique.

"You guys would still have to share a room. And the ceilings are low and it's not very friendly. I don't like it. It has gas heat. We would have to keep it cold."

"How do you know it has gas heat?"

I pointed impatiently to the closet beside the bathroom. "Gas furnace equals gas heat."

"You notice the oddest things, you know that? I mean, you don't know not to wear your slippers in the rain, but you notice in a glance whether or not a house has gas heat. How do you do that?"

I shrugged impatiently. "I guess different things just seem important to me than they do to other people."

"No kidding," Lanie called from the bathroom, where she was standing in the tub, no doubt imagining showers to come.

I used to be like Lanie. As recently as last week, in fact. Ordinarily, I loved looking at vacant houses with signs in their yards. They were so hopeful when we met them, each with a slightly different set of promises to make. I loved to walk through the empty rooms, listening to the echo of my footfalls, knowing it would be muted later by the presence of boxes, then clothing, odds and ends of furniture, and the voices of my sisters and the comforting sounds of living.

This house being on Pendleton Street, I should have loved it more even than the others. But something was wrong with the idea of this house. It was too small for our family, which felt bigger by the day as I grew taller, as the pressure got more insistent. And it wasn't the Sun House, so it wasn't going to do.

Lanie was staring at me with a puzzled expression on her face.

"Who died?" she asked flatly when I met her gaze.

It took me a moment to work out what she meant. "Do I look sad?"

She nodded uncertainly. "You do."

I did something then that I didn't do very often: I made my facial expression into a lie. Forcing a smile at Lanie, I stretched out a hand for her. "This one's too small," I said as she uncertainly took my hand. "Let's start looking for another." I pulled her with me onto the front porch and began scanning the lawns for a sign.

Chapter 11

The air outside was crisp and colder than it should be, two days before November. Lanie's hand in mine was warm and I remembered her being little, remembered the last time I felt bigger than her. Some years had passed since then.

I started to pull her toward the Sun House, but she pulled back just as insistently.

"Not a chance," she said with a shiver. "Uh-uh."

So we headed right instead. Little rocks rolled under my shoes and made it difficult to walk as fast as I suddenly felt I needed to. One street over from Pendleton was Probart. I tugged my sister in that direction, terribly curious about something Mrs. Rhodes said the day before.

The angle of the back porch meant it had to be

the house on the left. The house's left, that is, not mine. It didn't take long to find them, either. It's not every day you see a sixty-five-year-old substitute teacher playing Ultimate Frisbee with her brother in the yard.

"Go long!" she shouted, and Otis Andrews did, sprinting the length of the yard to grab the Frisbee out of the air.

"Yes!" Mrs. Rhodes squealed, jumping and clapping for her brother. I felt an odd sort of giggle bubbling up in my throat. I was pretty sure there was a rule about teachers and Frisbee and I was pretty sure she was breaking it, but I didn't have the words for it just yet.

"I've still got it, sis!" Otis Andrews announced in a proud sort of voice.

"That you do!" She was laughing. "Me, on the other hand . . ."

"Aah, come on, sis, you gotta try it!"

"All right, all right!" She winced and braced herself as he threw the Frisbee back. I noticed that it moved in a gentle pattern, exactly into her hands. I thought maybe that had more to do with Otis Andrews than with Mrs. Rhodes.

"Is her name 'Sis'?" I whispered to Lanie.

"I don't think so," she whispered back. "I think that's her brother. Do you know these people?"

"Oh. That's Mrs. Rhodes, my new substitute teacher, and her brother, Otis Andrews."

"Oh, well, see, he's calling her 'sis' like 'sister.' "

"Huh." That made sense, I guess. Crouching behind the porch railing, we watched them playing in their yard like two little kids.

"Do you think they know we're watching?" Lanie asked after a minute, and Mrs. Rhodes called from the yard, "Of course we do! We're old, not blind!"

Despite her words, I thought I saw Otis Andrews jump a little, and I suspected he hadn't been aware of us till then. The Frisbee stopped almost in midair, the way it sank into his grip, like he had called it.

"Well, hello there," he said, walking toward us.

"Hello." I felt my eyes get funny and slip away from him, not sure where to look.

"And how are you this fine afternoon?"

Since it was freezing cold, without even the decency to snow, I wasn't sure what he meant by "fine," but perhaps it was just something to say, like the chipped paint on the porch railing was just something for me to look at.

"Doing well, thank you," I said automatically, Natasha's manners drilled into me for years became habit. "And yourself?"

"Why, I'm splendid." From some people, it might

have sounded trite, just something to say, but the way he said it, I believed him.

"You're very good at Frisbee," Lanie said politely, while I hummed softly, just under my breath, hoping Otis Andrews wouldn't notice.

"Are you nervous, dear?" Mrs. Rhodes asked, noticing my humming just like she noticed everything. I kept humming without answering, because I didn't want to admit it and I also didn't want to lie.

"We were looking at a house," Lanie said. "She didn't like it, though."

"Oh, are you moving?"

"We got evicted." Lanie's head bobbed up and down. I was pretty sure you weren't supposed to tell people you got evicted, because usually they got embarrassed and stammered a lot and looked away. But Mrs. Rhodes just smiled.

"We've had those months, haven't we, Otis?"

Otis Andrews nodded politely. "And how," he agreed, although I wasn't quite sure what that meant.

"Would you like to play Frisbee?" Otis Andrews asked. "It's an original Wham-O forty mold, 1978."

"I'm not very good at Frisbee," I said tentatively, and hummed.

"We should be getting back," Lanie said quickly. "We were just looking for For Rent signs and we wandered a little far."

"House you were looking at wasn't up to par, then?"

"It was awesome," Lanie said at the exact same time as I said, "It was terrible."

"Houses are like that," Mrs. Rhodes said, not at all confused by our split reaction. "Picky about who they like. The trick is finding a house that likes the whole family. Right, Otis Andrews?"

"Quite right, sis."

"Well, you two young ladies have a fabulous day," Mrs. Rhodes said, and she waved us on our way, although I suspected she would stand at the corner and watch till we made it back safely.

We hadn't gone even a block when Lanie spotted Karen walking quickly down the sidewalk.

"Girls!" she hollered when she saw us. "Where have you been?"

"Looking for For Rent signs," Lanie said with a blush. "We didn't mean to go so far." She cast me an accusing glance.

"We were *at* a For Rent sign!" Karen said in exasperation.

"I don't like that one," I said faintly. "And I remembered that my teacher lived on Probart Street and I wanted to see."

"Your—the new sub?"

"Mrs. Rhodes and her brother."

Mom put her head in her hands for a moment. "Oh, Livvie, Lanie. You girls just can't go bothering a teacher at home!" She began leading us back the way we'd come, toward Mrs. Rhodes's house.

"They were outside, Mom, it's okay," Lanie said. "They were playing Frisbee."

Mom seemed to take this account with a grain of salt, a phrase Tasha used to mean *I doubt it*. "Whatever they were doing," she said sternly, "you can't just go barging into their personal lives like that. And, Livvie, how many times lately have you been told not to leave our sight without asking?"

"But I took Lanie." I glanced at Lanie and back at my mother, confused. "I didn't go alone."

"Lanie is not an adult. She's an eleven-year-old child. She's not allowed to wander off, either, Livvie, so you're definitely not allowed to take her with you! We talked about this just this morning and you made a promise! Livvie, you can't go breaking promises like this! How can I trust you?"

"Livvie, you broke another rule!" I hollered, and Lanie's face got red.

"Hush, they'll hear you."

"Who'll hear you?" I asked, although my wording didn't sound quite right.

"Mrs. Rhodes and Otis Andrews." Indeed, we were nearing their house.

They had taken a break from Frisbee to flop onto the lawn furniture, looking relaxed, although there wasn't a speck of sun in the sky.

"Why, hello again," Mrs. Rhodes said pleasantly as she saw us approaching. Standing, she extended her hand to my mother. "Vesta Rhodes. Olivia's new substitute, although I imagine she's told you that."

Mom smiled weakly. "I'm Karen Owen," she said. "I'm so sorry if they bothered you."

"They were absolutely no bother," Mrs. Rhodes said briskly. "You have lovely children. Why don't you come over tomorrow and not be a bother again? We have brunch on Sundays at ten-thirty."

Karen looked a little surprised, but Mrs. Rhodes's gaze was kind.

"Well . . . that would be lovely," Karen said uncertainly.

Otis Andrews stood suddenly, refusing to make eye contact with my mother. He gave me a crooked smile, so like his sister's. Nodding at me, he said, "I like this one, she's a funny one, this one."

Mom smiled at him, a look of realization dawning as Otis rocked from foot to foot. "That she is," she agreed.

Walking back to the rental house, I waited for my mother to fuss at me some more, but instead she only wrapped an arm around my shoulder and squeezed. She had to reach up to do it. I was taller than her, which I thought was an awfully strange thing, since she was a grown-up and I felt very far from it.

We made it back to the house just as Simon locked up. I could tell at a glance that Karen hadn't mentioned to him we were missing; he looked more relaxed and happy than I had seen him in a while. Behind him, Natasha, too, looked happy. Happy enough I knew Simon would be calling the landlords when we got home, and Karen would pick up more boxes at work tonight. I tensed my shoulders.

"Is the neighborhood to your liking?" Simon asked when he saw us walking close.

"Can we walk this way and check?" I asked a little desperately, pointing toward the factory. Lanie elbowed me and I ducked away from her. I was struck with the idea that if I could get them all down to the Sun House, if I could remind them how happy we were there—maybe when they *saw* the For Rent sign—

But Simon was shaking his head. "Honey, your mom and I have to go to work this evening. Can it wait for another day?"

"I don't want to wait for another day, I want to show you."

"Livvie," Karen said quickly, "if we live on this

street, you'll be able to walk down to the factory every day. In the daylight. *With* permission."

"That's not where I want to walk to!" I hollered over my shoulder, already running. "Come on! It'll just take a second!"

"Dammit, Livvie!" Simon's voice followed me down the block and I sprinted faster. I heard feet behind me. Didn't know whose till Natasha caught me.

"Livvie, stop!" She took my arm, spun me midstep. "Stop running after something that isn't there! Just stop!"

"It *is* there!" I grabbed her sleeve and pulled her with me. "Why won't anyone look?" We were nearly there. I could see the factory gate in the distance, and, closer, the looming white walls that once shone bright yellow. "Just look!"

Natasha yanked her sleeve loose. Her cheeks were pink. "Liv, it's not going to happen!"

"But it's for rent, Tash! There's a sign! Come and see!" I ran without her, gravel scattering under my shoes. Behind me I could hear Simon's voice raised, could hear Natasha shouting. All that frustration. All that sadness behind me. If I could just get them to come with me, back to the Sun House, where they were so happy—if I could just get them to look—

My feet hit the steps at the same time Simon caught my sleeve.

"Olivia Owen!"

I tripped on the top step and sprawled out sideways across the rotting porch. Beneath me I could feel wet wood, soggy in a way that made my skin crawl. I smelled mud and something heavy and solid. Simon sat beside me so quickly I thought he must have fallen, too. He swore again under his breath.

"Liv—are you all right?" His face was red with worry and anger.

I turned over, rubbing skinned elbows, and let him help me sit up on the rotting wood. He was angry and upset and I knew I had messed up again. Between us lay the sign, facedown. Wordlessly, breathing hard, I plucked the wet cardboard up off the porch and pressed it into his hands. The corner tore a little in my grip, but the words were there. They were shaped funny, now that I was looking close.

"This," I finally said. "I wanted to show you."

He looked at it and the crinkles on his forehead got deeper. He was breathing hard from the chase and for a moment he didn't say anything. Despite the cold, he had sweat running rivers down his face. He turned away from me with a grimace. His face stayed red.

Behind us I heard the porch steps creak and knew Natasha had joined us. Lanie and Karen lingered at the street.

"Why?" Simon asked. "What's so important about

this sign that made you want to run away again like that?"

"Daddy, she can't read it," Natasha said, sinking down to sit beside us. "She doesn't know."

I looked from my sister, who had tears starting in her eyes, to my father, who had a hand on his forehead, frowning fiercely. Moving slowly to stand, I backed away from them, but I tripped on the rotting floorboards and had to catch myself on the doorknob.

The door swung open, but the smell that wafted out was nothing at all like fried potatoes. I saw lumber on the floor. Pipes sticking out of the wall. The furnace was gone, which meant my name was gone from the walls. There was a faint smell like heat, like a campfire after a rain. I tugged the door till it shut. Drew a breath. And turned.

"It doesn't say For Rent, does it?"

When Simon didn't answer, I looked at Natasha.

"It says Condemned," she said tiredly. "It means they're going to tear it down. Livvie, that's what I told you. We're never going to live here again."

Chapter 12

*T*ash was out with me and we were hand in hand, the way my mom preferred us to be when we were walking by the road, never mind the fact that I was fourteen and I knew about cars.

It was August, only two months before October but so different, and the sky was hot and heavy with storm. My mind tricked my feet into thinking they were happy and we walked the streets of Nabor with a bounce in our steps, absolutely certain we would find him today.

Cats didn't disappear, and they certainly didn't do it in a town the size of Nabor, where everybody knew whose cat was whose. Orange Cat would be perfectly safe here and I knew it. Now all I had to do was coax his stubborn self out into the open so I could catch him.

There was the finest mist of warm, soft rain starting to work its way down from the clouds. Tash looked
up into it and laughed, her hair blowing back as the
storm blew closer.

"I love storms," she laughed out loud into the sky.
"Bring it on! I've been waiting for it!"

"It's not going to come yet," I reassured her confi-
dently. "It's going to be an hour yet or more before it
comes."

"How can you tell?" she asked with a skeptical laugh.
Having been my sister for so long, she was nonetheless
not always certain when I was being definite and when
I was just making guesses.

"It just doesn't feel like it's ready yet," I said. "Trust
me. I'm sure of it. It might drizzle, but it isn't going to
storm till after three."

It was the last day before school started, the last
day before I had to commit myself to eight-hour days
of trying to fit myself into a mold I didn't understand
and had no use for. I really wanted to spend this last
hot August night of freedom with my Orange Cat. And
I really didn't want him out in the storm.

"Orange Cat!" I yelled into the wind, gleeful hope
picking up my step so I was dancing under the clouds
as we worked our way along Pendleton Street. "Come
back now, you silly thing! You've been gone three days
now! You've made your point!" Humming with glee, I

skipped a few steps. "You're going to be sorry if you stay out in the storm! You're going to wish you had listened and just come home when I first asked you!"

Beside me, Tash stopped walking and made a small sound in her throat.

The houses were small along this street, but they were familiar and I liked them. The yards stretched a little farther than on some streets, and they were filled with interesting things like clotheslines or gardens or leftover yard sale items. One house had six mailboxes, all in a row propped by the porch, like they were making them or selling them or saving them for something.

That's where my eyes were—on the mailboxes. My peripheral vision was something we had talked about at length, last school year. Sometimes I saw things differently there. Sometimes something I saw as huge or dark or scary out of my peripheral vision turned out to be commonplace once I faced it head-on. But this time it was different and I knew it.

He looked too pale, so I was certain it wasn't him. Who knew part of his orange came from the inside? Without the life inside him, he was only dull yellow. Tash grabbed my hand and started to cry.

But not me. I didn't cry as I yanked my hand free. I only walked toward him as my hands balled into fists, as my eyes refused to stay closed.

I couldn't look him in the eye because his face was messed up. Instead I took in his stomach and his paw pads and the rings around the tail, and even as my brain said no, I knew yes beyond a doubt. I was a girl who noticed details and I couldn't deny them now. I knew the weight, the color, the specific slant of his patterns. As different as he looked in death, I knew who I was seeing.

The storm came then, just one thing more that I was wrong about.

No Sun House. No Orange Cat. Only cool colors left. The tantrum was like no other, at least not since the night Orange Cat died. Before I woke up enough to know what I was doing, I had already broken my alarm clock and ripped several pictures off the walls.

It was neither a scream nor a hum, the sound I was making, and it took me a long time to realize who was making it. When I realized it was me, I tried to stop it, but the pressure was exploding behind my eyes and slamming into my stomach and it was either scream or explode, so I exploded. My hands flew into my hair and I began to rock wildly, yanking at my hair while my back thumped against the wall over and over.

I was barely aware of my mother arriving, her

hands tugging uselessly at mine. Then my father, stronger and more determined. Suddenly he was holding my hands instead of my hands holding my hair.

I fought him, flinging my head forward to catch him in the chin, then scratching at his fingers with my nails. The whole time, I was horrified at my own behavior. I didn't want this to be happening. But I needed the pressure to stop and he wasn't letting me make it.

I knew my parents were talking, shouting, but I couldn't hear them over the whooshing in my head, over my own strangled screaming. I heard something crack the next time I flung myself into the wall, and I knew I had lost us our damage deposit, if it wasn't lost already. Funny the clear bits of sky that could appear in the midst of a storm.

Simon gathered me up again, holding so tight I couldn't move. After a minute, the tight hold began to feel comforting, as though the pressure from the outside was reversing the pressure from the inside.

As soon as the screaming was gone, it was replaced by tears. This was something new. I almost never cried during a tantrum. But as soon as the screaming was gone, the dream had a chance to come back. I wrapped my arms around Simon's neck and sobbed, terrified he wouldn't hug me back, terrified I had just done something irreversible.

Simon shushed me and rocked me as he had when I was small, while Karen's hands stroked my hair and her soft voice soothed me.

When my eyes could focus, they focused on Natasha, holding Lanie's hand in the doorway. Funny, I could hear my parents, but I still couldn't hear my sisters. It struck me nervously that maybe they weren't talking.

"I'm sorry," I started saying, mostly to fill the void of my sisters' silence. "I'm sorry. I'm sorry." Over and over. So many times I didn't notice feet approaching till Natasha was there beside me.

"Shush, Livvie," she said with a hint of firmness in her voice, sounding very much like our mother. "You're all right."

I was so tired right that second, I almost believed her on the surface. Underneath, I thought maybe I would never believe her. Underneath, I felt like my insides were shaking. I was scared. I didn't like this girl who kept throwing tantrums and breaking things. I wanted to get as far away from her as possible.

I rocked back hard against Simon. "Livvie, stop this!" I demanded. "You're ruining everything!"

Simon shook his head against me. "You're not ruining anything, baby. You just need to calm down."

"I can't. That's why I'm ruining everything!" I sniffled, switching at last into first person. "I can't calm down when everything is so hard! I can't calm down, Simon!"

"Ssssh." He continued to rock me against him. "Ssssh." His hands stroked my hair, his lips brushed my forehead, and despite my words, I found myself beginning to relax.

"That's my girl," he whispered. "That's my Livvie-bug."

"Am I?" I ventured after a very long moment.

"Oh, hush," he said like Karen. "You always will be."

These were the words, at last, that made it possible for me to relax, still wrapped in my father's arms. He eased me back into my bed and pulled up my nine blankets, taking care to get them even. Karen kissed my forehead, then turned Lanie by the shoulders and headed her back to bed. Simon was left to straighten my torn-up pictures, to right my fallen lamp.

Tasha slid into bed beside me and propped herself up against the pillows. Her hand reached around me to pluck one of my old favorite books off the nightstand.

"What are you doing?" I asked with sleep in my voice. Now that I was calm, I felt heavy, like I was sinking down into the bed and getting swallowed by the pillows.

"I'm visiting an old friend," she answered, her voice sounding very far away. She began to read, words coming alive and drifting dreamily off the page, and I sank into sleep almost at once.

Chapter 13

I woke in the night, but for the first time in a long time, it wasn't the whistle that did it. Playing sounds back in my head as I drew on my night sweatshirt and stuck my socked feet in my sneakers, I knew the step that had stolen down the hall. The only question now was why. Why would Lanie Owen, ever sensible, be sneaking out at this hour?

I slipped past Tasha, asleep with her book on her chest. I knew which sections of carpet to avoid, which would give me away with their creaking. Good thing Lanie hadn't known. Outside, the November air was bitter and my breath was snatched away almost the minute I stepped out. I took the wooden steps carefully, wary of the frost, and at the bottom, I found one footprint blackening the grass between the bottom step and the gravel of the driveway. I could still hear her footsteps fading away.

"Wait," I whispered into the darkness. Then, when the sounds kept fading, "Lanie, *wait!*"

In the darkness, I wasn't sure, but then I came across her waiting. She stood with her hands cupped in front of her and tears running down her cheeks. In the darkness, in the night, without a bit of mean or angry in her, she looked much younger than eleven. Much younger than her big sister, too, for the first time in a while.

The emotions on her face had no name, but I knew it wasn't just me this time. No one had a name for this, although we all felt it some horrible night.

Gently uncupping Lanie's hands, I found Bentley cradled in them. He was grayer tonight, the part that made him the whitest gone forever. I kept my hands under him and leaned my forehead against hers.

We stood like this perhaps longer than any other two people might have done. Then I whispered, "Where are you taking him?"

Lanie sniffled and gulped huge. "I don't know," she said in a small voice. "I'm just . . . taking him."

I took her hand then and tugged her with me. "Come on, then."

"Where—"

"Don't argue with your big sister," I said firmly. "Trust me, Lane."

She did, cradling Bentley's small body to her chest with her free hand. Tears continued to slip down her cheeks, but she didn't argue with me, following me through the darkness as if she trusted me. It was a great responsibility, but I knew at once I could handle it. We stole through Nabor-with-an-A for what I knew would be the last time at this particular hour, deliberately skipping Probart Street for safety's sake. Mrs. Rhodes would only mean well, but she mustn't stop us this time.

There was a car in front of the Pendleton Street rental house, and boxes on the porch. In a few hours' time, we had missed our chance for that one. I heard Lanie sigh in the darkness and then she sniffled again, harder. As difficult as it was for her, losing her little mouse friend and science partner, I knew that wasn't the only sadness running down my sister's cheeks.

The Sun House looked softer tonight than it had in the day. I wasn't even scared as I led Lanie up the broken front walk, up the wooden steps onto the porch. There we sat, backs against weathered wood that remembered us well, no matter how little and how different we had been, all the way back then.

I couldn't smell the heat or the water from here,

but I had memories, the kind you aren't sure you're really remembering until they keep drifting up in your head the same way. I remembered me and Tash with our blankets, me and Tash trying to light the fire on the wall while Karen and Simon were still asleep. I thought maybe the fire escaped from its box. I thought maybe I remembered the way the water looked in the air as it was spraying, and then we left like the paper mill and didn't come back.

Someone must have tried to fix up the place, after. Painted the walls. Took out the gas furnace. But the Sun House was never the same after that.

"I don't remember this place," Lanie whispered, "but I kind of do, you know?"

"It remembers you, too," I promised, reaching for her mouse. I took off my sneaker and sock, then replaced the sneaker and helped Lanie wrap her little mouse in my sock. "It's clean, more or less. I promise."

She laughed through her tears. "He doesn't care."

I hummed for a minute and rocked, taking Lanie in my arms so she rocked with me.

"Is this . . ." Lanie ventured in a small voice after a moment. "Is this how you've been feeling, Liv? Like it's your fault, about Orange Cat?"

I nodded. "Orange Cat and other stuff, too. Only

Mrs. Rhodes said it isn't. And Tash said it isn't. And Karen and Simon said it isn't. And guess what?"

"What?"

"It *isn't*."

Lanie sniffled. "You promise?"

"Livvie doesn't lie. Not much."

Lanie giggled a little through her sniffling. Then went quiet again. "I hope he was happy," she said, and sighed. Her voice drifted off across the weathered old porch, blending into the creaking of the doorway and the distant laughter I might have just imagined. My fingers picked at wet old wood and bits of it came apart in my hand. My bracelet caught on the splinters and Orange Cat's collar fell away. I caught it with my fingertips and rubbed the brass tags that had become so worn.

"He looked happy, he looked really happy," I finally said. "He got to be in science fairs and he got to sit on the kitchen table when Karen wasn't looking. And he did his job good, just like Orange Cat."

Lanie looked at me funny. "What do you mean, his job?"

"He was supposed to be happy and get you a scholarship, and he did."

"Then what was Orange Cat's job?"

"To teach me," I admitted, feeling more clear than I had in a while.

She gulped again. "And did he?"

"Yep." I stroked her hair and wiped the tears off her cheeks with my thumb. "He taught me."

We sat together on the porch, rocking and humming Bentley's favorite song, which Lanie insisted was the theme from *Star Wars*. And *I* was supposed to be the odd one. When it was finished, Lanie swallowed and sat up straighter.

"He wants to stay here," she said. "He wants to be buried here, where we started." It was the sort of thing I might have said, and the whisper-soft way she said it, I knew she noticed.

"I know he does," I said as my hands slid Orange Cat's collar back and forth between them.

We buried them along with the Condemned sign, digging in the dirt with broken timbers from the porch. Lanie began to cry again as she placed Bentley into the ground and covered him with the soft earth of our first home. I stroked Orange Cat's collar as though there were someone inside it. Then placed it in a hole not much bigger than Bentley's, touching the worn tag one last time.

"Bye, buddy," I whispered.

"Bye, buddy," Lanie echoed like the child she was, and we patted the cold earth together.

The stars were starting to fade by the time we stood, dusting the dirt from our pajamas, to begin the walk home. Hand in hand, we walked slowly, not nearly as worried as we should have been about being caught or getting in trouble. We had simply let go of too many things tonight to worry about anything else.

It began to rain and my second set of pajamas started to get ruined. My one remaining sock was getting muddy and I knew my sneakers would be crispy for days. There was a thick kind of sadness in my head, and a lot of responsibility that came with Lanie's hand in mine.

There was no pressure, though. I had buried all that with Orange Cat's collar and my sister's little mouse. At least for now.

"I'm cold," Lanie said as we passed Probart and started up Main. So I told her about the gas furnace, the way you lit it with a switch on top, the way I'd recorded my name on the blackened metal because it was the warmest spot in the house. As we shivered our way through the dark air, I told Lanie all about the start of our lives, in the warmth and the safety of the Sun House. I had been waiting for ten years to tell somebody the whole story, and the words poured out almost all in the right order. As our toes grew colder in the frozen grass, I drew the Sun House all around us. The sun itself had started over the mountains by the time we came in sight of home.

"Now, now Livvie's left something even better than a name on the wall," I boasted proudly, humming a little. "Now Lanie and Livvie each left something wonderful."

We stopped talking as we crept past the mailboxes into the trailer park. Janna's trailer was the only one lit, and I heard her TV faintly as we passed. Miraculously, our trailer was still. We climbed the frosty steps, crisscrossing our outgoing footprints with our incoming ones, and I showed Lanie how to lift the front door so it wouldn't creak. A glance through our parents' bedroom door revealed that they were both still asleep, exhausted from all the worry last night.

"When it's later," I whispered to Lanie as I walked her to her door, "I need your help with something, okay?"

"Okay." Her eyes got smaller. I think the look there was called *suspicion*. Another one I had some experience with. But she was too tired and sad to ask about it.

I tucked her into bed and kissed the top of her head the way Karen was always doing. She shivered at my cold touch and sniffled.

"Hey, Liv?" she asked just as I was about to slip out the way I'd come.

"What is it, Lane?"

"Do you want me to come fix your blankets?"

I giggled, not quite sure why. Then fixed Lanie's blanket instead, tucking it in so it would be heavy. She sank down under it and her eyes started blinking. I started thinking I could make her go to sleep all cozy, just like Tasha had done for me earlier. Sliding a book off the shelf, I struggled through a few words and drew up short.

"It's okay," she mumbled, shoving the book away. "Just tell me instead."

So I told her my newest plan.

Chapter 14

This time the house was peaceful, and someone had swept up the clutter off the floor. There was nothing hot or wet about the place. Everything was dry and pleasantly warm. The floorboards shone with a sweeping and a mopping and the sun poured in at all angles like it used to. There were moons in the shutters, though. No one had fixed those yet.

We were little, and I knew this was right for this house. I was so little I couldn't reach the counter, and Lanie was a baby in a crib. But Orange Cat was there, as usual, stalking silently through the house, glowing as bright orange as I had ever seen him.

He led me to the bedroom, his purr so loud I could have followed it with my eyes closed. The familiar food dish in the corner of the room was overflowing, and Orange Cat sat gently on his haunches to eat a few bites. His purr stayed loud, wavering a little with his crunching. I knelt on my bedroom floor and reached out a hand to stroke him.

He let me, and I knew that this was it. This was the last time I would see him.

"I'm sorry," I whispered, but the way he looked at me, I knew there was no need. He didn't blame me.

Leaving his dish, Orange Cat hopped lightly onto my knees the way he used to. Bumping his face against my cheek, he happily claimed me.

Then he leapt delicately from my lap and returned to his food dish. There was laughter in the house and I knew it was time for me to go. The laughter and the yellows and the oranges I had missed would still be safe here, even after I was gone. Even though I would never come back.

"You want to talk about it?" Natasha was sitting on the end of my bed, holding Gray Cat and scratching her chin, when I woke up the next morning.

I stretched and yawned, feeling a slight ache in my back from my tantrum last night. It seemed a million years ago. I knew that was what Natasha meant, though.

"Do *you* want to talk?" I asked uncertainly. "We haven't done much talking lately. I think that Livvie is on your last nerve."

Natasha slumped a little. "No, she isn't. I'm just scared for her because I don't know why she's been so stressed out lately."

I stretched my feet comfortably to the end of the bed and arched my back. With a long sigh, I shook my head.

"I'm not stressed out now," I said.

"Well . . . good, then." She looked confused, but not unhappy, and when I smiled, she giggled out loud. "You're so funny."

We sat for a minute, petting Gray Cat between us. Then I sat straight up in bed as my plan came flooding back.

"Hey, Tash," I said. "Has the trash run yet?"

She gave me a puzzled look. "I have no idea."

Ten minutes later, we sat on the end of Lanie's bed, spreading real estate ads between us. This time it wasn't the For Sale section we looked at. And it wasn't in Nabor-with-an-A. The crinkled sections of paper I usually threw away, we now smoothed so my sisters could read them.

"Here's a good one!" Lanie squealed, and Natasha and I shushed her.

"Do you want Mom to hear?" Natasha whispered. "Keep it down!"

"But look at this!" Lanie whispered excitedly. "That's a good price, isn't it, Natasha?"

Natasha looked, then circled the ad. "I'll get the phone," she whispered.

The door opened before she could move, and I flung myself sideways to hide the classifieds. I also hid Lanie's feet by smashing them into the bed, and she shrieked and started tickling me.

Natasha plunked a pillow down on top of both of us, muffling our giggles. "That takes care of that," she said firmly.

Karen smiled from the doorway for a long moment before she spoke. "I hate to break this up," she prodded gently, "but if we're still going, Liv, we have to *go*."

Obediently I slipped out of the bed and headed for my room. I had nearly forgotten the invitation. Slipping my hand into Karen's, although I was too old for this, I cast my sisters a small wave and followed my mother out of the house.

Twenty minutes later, we sat on soft chairs, looking nervous at each other.

"I'm so glad you could come," Mrs. Rhodes said with a smile to my mother, offering her a plate of biscotti.

"Oh, thank you." Karen took one and dipped it in the hazelnut coffee Mrs. Rhodes had given her. I had a mug, too, surprisingly comforting though it wasn't made of mud, full of mostly milk and enough coffee to make it the right color.

I took a biscotti, too, and dipped it in my hazelnut milk. It tasted crunchy, so I soaked it longer and a piece of it fell off. Having soggy biscotti floating in your coffee is extremely unappetizing. I started to set my mug on the table, but I caught Otis Andrews watching me closely and I suddenly thought it would be rude not to finish my drink. Lifting it again, I took a slow sip. The soggy biscotti slipped onto my tongue and wriggled its way down my throat. I squished my eyes shut and hummed very quietly.

When I opened them, Otis Andrews was still watching. He leaned in close.

"I don't like soggy stuff in my coffee, either," he whispered as though we were classmates trying to keep from getting caught by the teacher. He took my mug to the kitchen and returned a minute later with a fresh batch of hazelnut milk for me.

"Oh. Thank you!" I smiled at him uncertainly and took a sip of the drink. It was warmer than the one Mrs. Rhodes had made and I liked how it felt slipping down my throat. I felt instantly warm.

Mrs. Rhodes's home was very like her, matter-of-fact, yet warm and inviting. There was nothing extra or frivolous, but only because Mrs. Rhodes made each thing she owned seem like it served a purpose. The knickknacks of kitty cats, the framed photos she got from the antique store, the wall hangings that looked like a kid had crocheted them, each item in her home was equally loved and needed.

I was pretty sure Otis Andrews felt that way, too. I also thought maybe he made Mrs. Rhodes feel that way. It was a very balanced home and I liked it very much.

Karen chatted easily with Mrs. Rhodes about everything from Mrs. Rhodes's curtains to my schoolwork, and when we walked home later it was with a peaceful silence sliding back and forth between us.

"That was nice of her," she said at last, "to ask us to visit."

"It was nice of you to come," I said.

"Her brother's an awfully sweet guy," Karen said. "Talented, too. Did you see the murals?"

"Mm-hmm. Mrs. Rhodes has pictures of them above her desk at school."

"She decorated? Hmm."

"What?"

"Well, maybe that means she's going to stay for a while."

"I hope she's going to stay for a while," I said quickly. "She's a real nice lady."

"Really," Karen corrected me absently. She was still an English major, somewhere deep down under the Walmart apron.

"Mom," I said suddenly, serious enough that I started with what she preferred to be called, rather than her proper name. "Are we moving to Neighbor-with-an-E?"

"Baby, I don't know. I know the house on Pendleton Street was rented to a couple with one child. I'm not sure that landlord was ever truly comfortable with us."

"Because of me?" I ventured.

"Because of *us*." She cupped my face for an instant. "A family of five, with pets, is a gamble for any landlord. They don't know what good kids we have."

I snorted, even though it was bad manners. Then started us walking again. It was cold out and I wanted to get inside and hug my warm Gray Cat.

"Mom, what if we *do* move to Neighbor-with-an-E? Will things be better?"

Mom looked at me in surprise. "I thought you were dead set against it."

"I used to be."

"But . . . ?"

I turned us spontaneously onto Main Street and led us toward downtown, wondering if I could say all this while looking it in the eye. If I could make eye contact with the courthouse and still tell my mother what I meant to tell her, well, then it was meant to be.

The soft clatter of the clock above the hardware store made me sigh. I turned my gaze to the courthouse with its prideful dome-shaped windows.

"But Lanie and Tash shouldn't have to share a room anymore, and nobody should have to drive that far every day just to work at the stupid Walmart."

Karen kissed me on the hair and urged me to walk a little faster, zipping my coat as we did. "We're okay, Liv."

"Livvie is, too."

She looked at me for a long time when I said this, like she was willing it to be true.

"Not at first," I admitted. "I was upset at the idea of leaving Orange Cat's grave and I didn't want to leave my school or G. And this town. We grew up in this town. It is our childhood home."

She smiled softly. "You're still a child, Liv."

"Not as much of one as Lanie. And Lanie's not half as upset about leaving this place as Livvie is." I slipped safely back into third person, but even with my eyes on the courthouse, seeing the disappointment in its windows, I was able to finish my thought.

"I want Lanie to have her own room," I said, "like Otis Andrews does. All painted. Only hers would be painted with science stuff."

Karen smiled. "That's a sweet thought," she said, and she smiled at me in this Mom sort of way. "You're getting so grown-up, Olivia."

As we walked on down Main Street, I watched my mother's eyes. She took in the gas station where we had gotten ice cream every summer, and a few Octobers, as long as I could remember. She took in the courthouse lawn where Natasha performed violin, back before she stopped doing anything except reading. Took in the hardware store with its bell above the door, a bell that rang, much quieter than the factory whistle but nonetheless just as reliable, every eight a.m. and five p.m. for longer than my life.

"I have a secret," Karen confessed, looking at me with bright eyes. "It wasn't just for you I didn't want to leave this place. I grew up here, too, Livvie."

"You grew up in Ohio," I protested.

"No. I was a child in Ohio. I grew up here." She smiled sadly around her at the town. "I married my husband here and I watched my children learn to walk here. This is my home."

I placed my hand very firmly in my mother's. "*This,*" I said, very gently, "is Livvie's home."

Looking at me with misty eyes for longer perhaps than I would ordinarily let her, she smiled at last, this time not quite so sad.

"You're getting so grown-up," she repeated. We fell silent then and sort of peaceful.

Chapter 15

Be careful!" Karen called after us, and the three of us, just barely overlapping, hollered back, "We will!"

My sisters hooked me by the elbows and hurried me forward so I couldn't say anything else. Lying was hard. Much harder than just sneaking out in the middle of the night when there was no one awake to lie to.

Jamie met us at the U-Save in his older sister's Bronco.

"Good morning, ladies," he said pleasantly, flashing me a smile as I squished into the backseat beside his two huge yellow Labs. Lanie squished in beside me as the dogs began smelling my clothing with interest. Uncomfortably, I realized I should have changed clothes after petting the cat.

"Don't eat Livvie," I said, very quietly, to the Labs. They sniffed me suspiciously, but seemed to be in agreement for the moment.

"Seat belts on," Jamie called. "All aboard the Jamie Express, now pulling out of the station for Neighbor!"

"With an E!" I exclaimed, and Jamie and my sisters echoed it.

It was rare I rode in a car with anyone other than Simon or Karen, and it was especially rare that I did so without telling either of my parents. In fact, I was pretty sure this was the first time. But because it was Jamie and because Natasha and Lanie were with me, I did my best to relax as we bumped over the train tracks and cut east through the county, toward Neighbor-with-an-E.

Jamie turned on the radio as soon as we passed the tracks. "We start picking up the good station in a minute," he said as a blast of static burst out of the radio and made me smush my hands over my ears.

"That's too loud!" I shouted, rocking hard and humming. One of the yellow Labs looked at me reproachfully, and I scooted toward Lanie.

"Livvie, be polite," Natasha scolded. "Jamie's doing us a favor!"

"Sorry," I said quickly. "Jamie, could you turn that down, please? It's too loud."

"No prob, kid," Jamie said easily, cranking the volume knob backward a notch. His old car was from seventeen years ago and I liked studying the different ways the gears and the knobs and the gauges on the dash looked from the cars that were made these days.

Natasha unfolded the newspaper and scanned the ads Lanie had helped me circle.

"The first one is on Michigan Street," she announced. "It's one of the four-bedroom ones, so let's hope it's good!"

"Or at least not a trailer!" Lanie squealed, bouncing in excitement.

"Is your seat belt on?" Natasha demanded, suspicious when Lanie bounced so high her head bumped the ceiling and made a yucky sound against the sagging cloth.

"Yes," Lanie lied.

"No it's not," I said automatically.

"Well, I don't have room to fasten it. Livvie's squishing me!" Lanie protested.

"These dogs want to eat me," I shot back. "I don't want to sit right under their noses!"

Jamie laughed at this while Natasha told us to hush or she would kick us out right here.

"You would get in so much trouble!" Lanie protested, shoving me sideways into the dogs so she could dig the end of her seat belt out of the crack of the seat.

"Some days I don't care," Natasha said in warning tones. "Get your seat belt on!"

"I'm doing it! Geez!"

"You girls are worse than me and my brothers." Jamie laughed. "Hey, don't kill each other before we even get to Mickey D's!"

"We're going to McDonald's?" Lanie shrieked.

"It's too yellow," I protested.

"It is *not* too yellow!" Lanie cried in exasperation. Although she kept patting my arm, as though I were one of the yellow Labs, in her voice and her face she was back to normal today.

"We'll drive through," Jamie compromised.

"That's okay, we'll eat when we get home," Natasha said quickly, and Lanie groaned in dismay.

"Are you sure?" Jamie asked.

Casting a fierce glance at Lanie in the side view, Natasha nodded. "We'll be fine."

"I'm buying," Jamie offered.

"Oh! Natasha, I have science fair money," Lanie said, pulling a wad out of her pocket. My eyes widened. She had almost ten dollars stashed away. It was the longest I'd ever seen Lanie hold on to money.

"Oh," Natasha said. "Well, I guess we can. Lanie,

if you buy something for you, you have to buy something for Livvie, too!"

"I can wait," I said quickly, and Natasha looked at me in surprise. "It's too yellow," I repeated. I noticed Lanie glancing suspiciously out of the corners of her eyes, but I didn't say anything else. Jamie eased the car to a stop at the first red light and began singing along with the radio, some rambunctious country song.

The first house came before McDonald's, and it was yellow. It was the wrong yellow, though, a mustardy gold color sort of like McDonald's. I made Jamie drive past it without stopping.

"Livvie, you never know," Natasha protested weakly. "The inside might be nice." But she didn't look any more eager than I did to stop at the mustardy house on its crowded little street.

"Where's the next one?" I demanded.

"Kinely Street."

"That's the one with the fence," I announced, remembering my phone call with the soft-spoken woman who owned the Kinely Street house. "She says it's pet friendly and she loves"—I leaned a little farther away from the Labs and dropped my voice low—"cats."

"Next stop: Kinely Street!" Jamie announced in his train engineer voice, steering a bit crookedly around a pothole in the road. There were fewer of those, I realized, ever since we passed the first stop-light of Neighbor. I wrapped the fingers of both hands around the seat belt fabric as Jamie acceler-ated onto Kinely Street and bumped to a stop next to a blue-and-white trailer.

"You didn't mention that," Lanie said pointedly.

"Neither did she," I said, although I didn't mind trailers in the least as long as they had good bathtubs. Nudging Lanie, I followed her out of the Bronco, eager to escape the hungry stare of the giant yellow Labs in the back.

The trailer stairs creaked and the front porch sagged. I noticed a neighbor sitting on her front porch directly across Kinely Street, staring at us. When she saw me looking, she stood and shuffled to her top step.

"Are you going to move in?" she called, which seemed premature, considering we had just pulled up. "I hope you're a quiet bunch. My husband's a day sleeper." Never mind she was bellowing across the road in the middle of the day.

"We haven't made any decisions yet," I called across to her, and began to hum. I didn't like her stare or the way her eyes went narrow.

"Actually, we have," Lanie said protectively, step-ping in front of me. "Time for Mickey D's, right?"

She led us back to the car and opened the door for me. The yellow Labs looked glad to see me back.

The McDonald's was next to a Wendy's and a Taco Bell. I didn't know Neighbor had so many restaurants and I wasn't sure what to make of it. Each indulged too much in its own overwhelming, neon-bright color: McDonald's in yellow, Wendy's in orange, and Taco Bell in purple. Despite my distaste at the decorating scheme, my stomach growled and I scooched a little closer to the yellow Labs so Lanie wouldn't hear it. Jamie swung the Bronco into the drive-through behind a family in a Pontiac and began tapping his fingers on the wheel in time to the music from an advertisement for Schick razors.

"May I take your order?" he said dramatically to Lanie, and she crossed her eyes and giggled, then passed nine dollars to the front. "Three double cheeseburgers, two with no onions and pickles and the other with no pickles and extra onions. Three small fries. And a medium diet soda."

My eyes fixed on Lanie in surprise. That was too much food for one eleven-year-old. That was also almost all of her money.

"Lanie," Natasha scolded. "You didn't have to get me anything."

Lanie snorted. "Maybe they're for the dogs," she

said, but when the greasy bags were handed through the window, she distributed them accordingly.

My sandwich had pickles on it even though she had asked for none. I scraped the onions off the pickles and gave the pickles to the Labs, who licked their lips and scooted closer to me, eyeing me in a way that made me hunch over my sandwich protectively. It had been ages since I'd had restaurant food and the burger was warm and delicious. I ate it in four quick bites as Lanie watched me skeptically.

"Don't choke," she said firmly. "Mom will know something's up if we get home and you've choked to death."

"Good point," Jamie said, and turned to me. "Remember what Mrs. Rhodes says?"

"Your food isn't going to get up and walk away, so slow down," I recited, then eyed the Labs. "Except my food really might get up and walk away. Right down these dogs' throats."

"Amber. Christina. Lay down," Jamie commanded, and the dogs happily ignored him and kept their eyes trained on my fries.

The fries were salty and crisp with an underlying sweetness that made me close my eyes and sigh deeply. *This* was bliss. The sweet warmth of McDonald's fries, long absent from my diet, had been missed, but never forgotten.

"You look like you're about to fall over," Lanie said, elbowing me. "Is it that good?"

I smiled blissfully. "Better!"

She smiled back like she just couldn't help it and I saw something new in her eyes. "Good," she said.

The third house on our list was on Lilly Avenue, and the inside smelled like mildew. Natasha took one step inside and stopped so quickly I immediately stepped on her heel.

"Ow," she said flatly.

"Sorry." I stepped back, right onto Lanie's toe.

"Ow!" Lanie shrieked.

"Sorry!" I said again, starting to get flustered.

"It's okay," Natasha said quickly. "This one won't do. It stinks."

"Couldn't we clean it?" I asked, starting to feel my hopes slipping away. There was only one more house on our list and at the rate we were going, we were still going to be homeless by the time the day was done. I was even starting to wonder whether we would have to go back and look at the Mustard House.

Jamie circled the block and pulled through the last stoplight in Neighbor. Two blocks later, he turned left onto Crab Orchard Drive. Crab Orchard wound along the creek and crossed over a tiny bridge. I felt a little pressure ease. I liked the way the trees watched us here.

"Three eighty-seven," Natasha said, peering again at Lanie's scribbled notes from the phone call she had helped me with.

Three eighty-seven Crab Orchard Drive was marked by a mailbox and a long gravel driveway. Jamie pulled the Bronco into it and we crept slowly up the rutted drive. Halfway up, we saw that Crab Orchard looped around so it passed the property closely on the side, but on the other three sides, the house was private.

Something started to snag at my memory and suddenly I felt like I was wearing wet slippers. The slippers took me back to the bus bench, and the bus bench took me back to the bus, a decade ago.

"The bus came here," I said abruptly.

Natasha looked around at me as we climbed out of the Bronco. "What are you talking about?"

I pointed to the loop of Crab Orchard. "It must have come there."

"How do you know?"

Because I knew the house, but I was speechless and couldn't tell her. It was a gentle brick. Orange brick. It had moons carved into the shutters. I knew the house, all right.

Something streaked across my vision and ran to hide under the porch. All that was left in my line of vision was a calico tail poking out. Somehow I knew that the animal who owned the tail also owned this empty house.

Right then, all the pressure went out of me and I grabbed my sisters' hands.

"This is it," I said, and we stepped forward.

Chapter 16

I smelled the paper, more solid than ever, while we sat on the bench and waited for the bus to come.

"You're all right, Livvie-bug," my mother promised when the bus's staring eyes made me afraid. She and Tash took my hands and guided me on despite my protests.

"Don't, don't, don't."

But we did, and it wasn't so bad once we were on. Immediately, I turned and sat on my knees so I could stare out the window as the trees rolled past. The bus swept a turn around the factory, where workers trailed back and forth with their hard hats and their lunch pails, hollering over the factory noise and laughing out loud about things like football.

I was little, but I understood laughing. I mimicked it and Karen ruffled my hair. The bus drew us down

Pendleton Street and turned left onto Main, chugging past the bank and the gas station and the hardware store. The courthouse, still open back then, winked in a friendly way as we bounced past it. The bus beeped and I put my hands over my ears, but Tash tugged them away and said, "Look who we're stopping for!"

It was a little girl my own age and she bounced onto the bus in a way that was familiar. I had never met the girl, but she bounced right up to me and sat down next to me, and I started humming G notes. Our mothers started talking, but neither one of us listened. I showed her how to sit on her knees like me, and we watched the streets of Nabor-with-an-A slip by as the bus picked up speed.

I didn't know any of the other houses in Nabor well, not back then. Still, certain ones seemed to be calling for my attention. A white one with shutters. A blue-and-white trailer. As we drew toward the end of Nabor, my eyes caught on the entrance to a trailer park and I watched it all the way past. Something made me hug my arms as I watched. The little girl be-side me mimicked me and squealed.

The bus seats were plastic covered in fabric, and they rug-burned my knees through the sweatpants I liked to wear. All the way to Neighbor, I felt the fabric burning my knees, but I didn't want to move. I liked the kid next to me and the way she bounced at every little thing. We didn't have to talk to have a conversation. Her little hands pointed every which way and my eyes went dizzy trying to keep up with all her observations, but in a good way. When she bounced off the bus at the first stoplight in Neighbor, she waved wildly and I flapped my hands at her and shrieked out a giggle. Mom laughed, watching us.

"You made a friend, Livvie," she said happily. "I'll have to give her mother a call."

The bus chugged us through six more stoplights and swung left onto Crab Orchard Drive, the back way in to the old Walmart, the one that wasn't as big. Though my friend was gone, I still stayed stuck to the window, unable to turn away. Houses slipped past by the creek and I liked to watch them with their friendly faces. One had pink-and-yellow curtains in checkers. Another had moons cut into the shutters. That one waved at me like the trailer park had done, and I waved back shyly.

"Who you waving at, bug?" Tash asked. When I didn't know how to answer, she lifted her hand and waved, too. "Hi, house!"

"Hi, house!" I echoed. "Hi, house, hi!"

"Hi, house!" Tash began to giggle and we waved together at the house as it slipped out of sight.

We had grilled cheese sandwiches for lunch at the diner, and drank milk out of mugs that felt like they were made out of mud. My parents laughed back and forth over our heads and Tash taught me a finger play about a church and a steeple and all the people inside.

The day was long, much longer than a tired four-year-old could manage, and I fell asleep on the bus heading home. I woke as the bus chugged onto Pendleton Street. It must have been six, because the mill whistle blew, attaching itself to the memory of the perfect day I'd had. Forever, the whistle would conjure up bus rides and grilled cheese sandwiches, mugs as smooth as mud and the house with the moons in the shutters.

Simon carried me off the bus and put me on my feet and I tensed, still sleepy and not sure where we were.

"It's okay, Livvie," Simon told me, and he showed me on the mailbox, where curly letters danced among pastel flowers. "We're back home, see? Simon, Karen, Tash, and Livvie Owen live here." I traced the letters with my fingers for a moment.

Then Simon steered me inside and sat me at the table while Karen lit the fire in the firebox. I heard the soft clicking and smelled the gas. It was the first cold night in Nabor that year and Karen hadn't lied. We were all right.

Chapter 17

Even though none of my classmates liked hugging, I felt the need to hug them when they offered to help me throw a party for Tash on Monday.

I attacked Michael first. Hugging Michael was like hugging Lanie's book bag with all the pens and pencils. He was all sharp points. He squirmed free and straightened the collar of his polo. He was less concerned with hugging than with the idea that there might still be snakes in the science lab at Tash's new school, and if there were, could she send him a picture.

Bristol came next. Even though she didn't like me, she liked Tash so much that, when I told her Tash was switching to the high school in Neighbor-with-an-E, she put her blue sweater on over all her warm colors. I hugged Bristol more for Bristol than for me, because that's what you're supposed to do when someone's sad. But Bristol was only sad for a minute before she started hollering orders to Robert, who was pulling chairs into the kitchen so there would be enough for the party. Hollering orders always made Bristol wear warm colors again, and off came the sweater after a moment.

G hugged me six or seven times, till I thought my ribs would crack. I kept telling her it wasn't me who was leaving, it was Tash, but she kept on hugging me, anyway. When I asked her why, she slapped a picture onto her Velcro of a beaming cartoon face with its stick hands clasped over its heart. Relief.

"Me, too," I admitted. "Livvie's re—I'm relieved, too."

When I first told G about moving to Neighbor-with-an-E, at the end of last week, she got this look on her face like maybe she wanted to dig out her picture of a cartoon frownie face. But I was beaming so big, I couldn't figure out why. She looked at me without saying anything for so long that I backed up a step and started rocking on my heels. My beam got less bright.

When she finally put the frownie face on the Velcro, it had a picture of me in front of it and I knew it was a question: *Won't you be sad?*

That got me started wondering if I *would* be sad

221

to leave Nabor High School, and once I started thinking about that, I couldn't think about anything else. I asked Simon when I got home that day whether G could come with me to Neighbor-with-an-E, and whether I was really going to have to leave Mrs. Rhodes right when I finally found Mrs. Rhodes.

Simon put the half-empty saltshaker he was about to pack down on the table and let the old newspaper he was wrapping it in drift back down into the box. He looked me square in the eyes, and even though that usually made me squirm, this time I met his gaze steady and waited.

"Absolutely not," he said without hesitation. "You're not switching schools, Liv, unless you want to. We'll get your principal to agree to it at your next meeting, and I'll drive you to Nabor High just like I used to drive Lanie to Neighbor-with-an-E. Problem solved." He dusted his hands as if there was an imaginary problem he was dusting away, though all there actually was was salt.

That was when relief happened. It was only later I realized that he just said me. Not Tash.

I spent most of the week refusing to think about it, because I wasn't sure what to think. But on our last morning living in Nabor-with-an-A, I blurted out the whole story to Mrs. Rhodes. And Mrs. Rhodes, of course, helped me find a way to manage things.

"Cream cheese makes a good chip dip for a party," she announced, banging things out of the cabinet. "That sister of yours, we'd better tell her good-bye before she rushes off to greener pastures."

"There's no pastures at Tash's new school, there's just a parking lot and it has eighty-eight parking spaces," Michael informed her. "I went there for summer school and they had snakes in the science lab. Do you think they still have snakes in the science lab? The black snake ate a *Mus musculus*. That's the proper name for a mouse."

"Well, Tash is leaving us for greener parking lots, then," Mrs. Rhodes allowed. Then, "Michael, sometimes it's best not to tell a girl if her new school has too many snakes."

We tricked Tash into coming to her surprise going-away party by sending her a note from Mrs. Rhodes that was written in Official Teacher Language. Bristol read it aloud to us before she and Mr. Raldy went to deliver it.

"Please send Natasha Owen to Mrs. Rhodes's classroom at your con—at—"

"—At your convenience," Mr. Raldy said, with what I was pretty sure was a hint of a smile, and the two of them went off together. Mr. Raldy was more interested in doing things around the classroom now that Otis Andrews seemed to be threatening to take his job. Otis had arrived as a volunteer at the end of last week and did not appear interested in leaving any time soon.

While the note was being delivered, the rest of us scrambled to make the classroom right. Michael busied himself hanging pictures of snakes, since he couldn't think of anything prettier to look at. G helped Mrs. Otis get the chips and the cups out on the table. Even Robert helped, thrilled by the privilege of standing on a chair long enough to hang the banner he and Bristol had written in marker on giant paper:

WE'LL MISS YOU, TASH!

Otis Andrews had read it out loud to me while he and Peyton drew swirls and sparkles around the letters, Otis sliding the paper under Peyton's marker while Peyton squealed with delight at the colors. Peyton hadn't stopped gazing at our new volunteer since his arrival. She got so excited making the banner that she moved her chin and her chair followed Robert all the way to the wall to hang her artwork. Now that the banner was hanging, she was watching Otis Andrews spin his Frisbee on his finger. She kept looking at me and back at the Frisbee, like, *Are you seeing this?*

I ventured closer and touched just the very end of her soft hair. "I see it, Peyton. It's very cool."

The door banged open and I spun from Peyton to find Tash, sandwiched between Bristol and Mr. Raldy, with her eyes going from the banner to me and back to the banner again.

"What did you do?" she asked with sparkly eyes like she wanted to cry, but maybe not in a bad way. Used to be, when Tash came to my classroom, she said, "What did you do?" and it meant *What trouble are you in?*

I looked around at my classmates, the ones I didn't used to feel at home with. Michael had never stopped darting around the classroom, pressing pictures of snakes onto the wall with Scotch tape. It was beginning to look like we were living in a jungle or the snake room at the zoo. Bristol and Robert and Peyton were all beaming at their banner, while G laid out napkins at the place settings in the kitchen.

"I didn't do anything," I admitted. This time it was true. "I only told them you were leaving and the rest is their fault."

Tash laughed and hugged me. Then hugged each of my classmates in thanks, just as I had done.

Funny thing, though. They *let* her hug them. It made me want to hug them all again, but I figured they'd had enough hugs forced out of them for one day.

We settled at the table with Tash right at the corner by the sink, the corner that was usually mine. I scooted my chair down carefully to make room for my sister, and she let me heap her plate with chips and a giant spoonful of cream cheese. Tash ate more chips than anybody, which made me think maybe she felt happy, like when I ate too much popcorn because movies were fun.

"Are you happy you're leaving?" I asked her while she helped Mrs. Rhodes clean the plates off the table. It struck me as wrong that she should help clean up the plates when the party was for her in the first place, so I took them from her and finished. I noticed the look she and Mrs. Rhodes exchanged.

"Liv, I really am," Tash said in answer to my question. Then she added quickly, before my feelings could get hurt, "I'll miss seeing you at school, though. It'll be different only seeing you at home."

I thought of the looks she'd had on her face the few times she did see me at school. Embarrassed. Uncertain. Sad.

"I think I'm happy, too," I told her. "I like how happy looks on you best."

She hugged me closer than all the others, and whispered something in my hair. I stepped back so

I could hear it and she met my gaze with a wide smile.

"Thanks. You're a good sister, Livvie."

Bright orange streaks worked their way up from the sunset by the time we reached the trailer to finish packing. Gray Cat firmly protested the idea of being packed, but I tricked her into her carrier with catnip and latched the door securely behind her.

"I'll take her," Natasha said, urging Lanie out the door in front of her. They had been in the middle of a heated argument that had a lot of smiles in it, for an argument. Natasha shouldered the strap of Gray Cat's duffel carrier and edged her out the door. "I know you have stuff to do!" she added over her shoulder.

But Lanie looped around, shouting, "Wait!" She began banging about the kitchen, checking cupboards to see that they were empty, so I figured I had a few moments before I had to finish up. Galloping out the door behind Natasha, I cut through the side yard and plunked myself on the ground next to Orange Cat's grave.

"I made you a memorial," I said. "It's on Pendleton Street, where we lived way back when. I'll come visit you there, okay?"

No one answered and the air stayed still, but I think maybe the sunset got oranger for a moment.

"I love you, too," I promised.

Lanie came banging out of the house, startling me into action. With a last kiss blown toward Orange Cat's grave, I galloped back into the house. I heard car doors slamming outside. Karen and Simon were trying to convince one last pillow to fit in the trunk, as Lanie and Natasha slid into the backseat, elbowing each other for a spot, but leaving space enough for me.

I closed all the doors in the house and locked all the windows, then ran each faucet one last time as if I could wash away the last of us. In this manner, I paced around the house, completing each of my leaving rituals with reverence. There were things that had to be done to make a house not ours anymore. It seemed so foreign, each time we moved, that this was the last time my hand would turn this hot water faucet with the missing H, that I would never again peer through the gathered dust of this particular window. It made sense to spend just a minute with each of these house parts I would never see again.

At last, all my rituals were completed except one, and I was ready. I even had the pen. It felt heavy with importance in my hand.

But I stood a moment, waiting. I wasn't sure for what until it happened. The whistle blew at exactly six o'clock, so quiet I knew I was the only one who could hear it. Just as it did, my eyes caught something purple on the kitchen counter, rolled halfway up under the microwave.

Stepping closer, I picked up my sister's purple pen. Then let my eyes wander to the white wall behind it. Something was written there in purple, and I knew all the words, but my brain took a moment before it pieced them all together.

Lanie Owen Lived Here, the wall said.

I smiled at my little sister's message for a moment while my throat closed up with an emotion I knew I wouldn't find on a flash card. At last, without writing anything, I dropped the pens on the counter for the next kid. As the whistle faded, I ran for the door, picking up speed as I hit the top step. In the car, my family waited. It was just after six and past time to head home.

Thank you for reading this FEIWEL AND FRIENDS book.
The Friends who made

Livvie Owen Lived Here

possible are:

JEAN FEIWEL, publisher

LIZ SZABLA, editor-in-chief

RICH DEAS, creative director

ELIZABETH FITHIAN, marketing director

HOLLY WEST, assistant to the publisher

DAVE BARRETT, managing editor

NICOLE LIEBOWITZ MOULAISON,
production manager

ALLISON REMCHECK, editorial assistant

KSENIA WINNICKI, publishing associate

ELIZABETH TARDIFF, designer

Find out more about our authors and artists and our
future publishing at www.feiwelandfriends.com.

OUR BOOKS ARE FRIENDS FOR LIFE